How to Write A Bestselling Werewolf Romance

Writing Werewolf Romances That Howl with Success

Just Bae

Contents

Introduction

Werewolf romance, a popular paranormal romance subgenre nowadays, captures readers' fascination with its unique blend of supernatural charm and romantic intrigue. At its core, the romance revolves around stories where at least one protagonist is a werewolf or shapeshifter who can transform into a wolf or wolf-like creature. This subgenre explores the primal, mystical aspects of its characters and delves into the complexities of their emotional and romantic lives. Unlike age-old romance novels, werewolf romances incorporate fantasy, horror, and mythology elements, offering a kaleidoscope of themes, including forbidden love, destiny, and the struggle between humanity and primal instincts. As a writer in this genre, you're invited to create worlds where the impossible becomes possible and where love transcends the ordinary boundaries of reality.

Within the paranormal romance genre, werewolf romance stories stand out for their exploration of pack dynamics and the inherent conflict between a werewolf's human and animal sides. These narratives often focus on the protagonist's dual nature, offering a metaphor for the internal battles we all face. You'll find that integrating this duality into your characters can deepen readers' emotional investment in their journeys. Themes of loyalty, belonging, and the search for identity are prevalent, resonating with readers drawn to finding one's place in the world, whether in human society or within the ranks of a werewolf pack.

One of the defining features of the werewolf romance genre is the mate bond, a powerful, unbreakable connection forged between two souls. This concept speaks to the genre's exploration of fated love and the idea that there is a perfect counterpart for everyone. In your writing, the development of this bond can serve as a central plot point, providing a rich ground for exploring themes of destiny, sacrifice, and the transformative power of love. The mate bond also introduces an element of certainty that challenges characters to embrace their true selves and the depth of their feelings.

These romances often include traits of danger and suspense, as the supernatural world is fraught with internal and external threats. Your stories can blend thrilling action sequences with heartfelt romantic moments, creating a dynamic narrative that keeps readers on the edge. The presence of adversaries, be they hunters, rival packs, or internal conflicts, adds layers of tension that can heighten the emotional stakes. This blend of action and romance is a hallmark of the genre, offering a compelling reason for readers to invest in your characters' journey.

Another aspect to consider is the role of the werewolf lore you choose to incorporate. The mythology surrounding werewolves varies widely, from cursed individuals to those who see their ability as a gift. By crafting your lore or drawing from classical myths, you create a backdrop against which your romance can unfold. This allows for flexibility in storytelling, where you can challenge conventional norms and introduce readers to a world rich with your own unique rules and traditions. Your interpretation of werewolf mythology can set your work apart, making it a distinctive contribution to the genre.

Writing a werewolf romance allows the writer to explore complex emotional landscapes. The transformation from human to wolf can metaphorize personal growth, change, and accepting one's darker, more primal side. Characters often grapple with issues of identity, control, and freedom, making for a deeply introspective and character-driven narrative. By focusing on the emotional and psychological aspects of the werewolf experience, you can create stories that are not only thrilling but also thought-provoking.

The setting is crucial, from secluded forests and mysterious small towns to bustling cities where werewolves hide in plain sight. Your choice of setting can significantly influence the atmosphere of your story, whether it's the eerie tranquility of a moonlit woodland or the chaotic energy of urban nightlife. Settings not only provide the backdrop for your narrative but also act as a character in their own right, reflecting and amplifying the themes of your story.

Social hierarchy and pack dynamics offer another layer of complexity in these romances. The structure of werewolf packs, with their alphas, betas, and omegas, can mirror human societal structures, providing a framework for exploring themes of power, leadership, and community. This aspect of werewolf lore allows for rich character development and plotlines centered around pack politics, leadership challenges, and the protagonist's role within or outside this hierarchy.

Along with the inclusion of rivalries and territorial disputes, these romances add an element of suspense and conflict. These elements often serve as a backdrop for the romantic plot, offering opportunities for the protagonists to demonstrate bravery, loyalty, and the strength of their bond. The tension between competing interests, whether between different packs or within a single pack, can drive the narrative forward, creating personal and communal stakes.

Know that the supernatural elements of a werewolf romance extend beyond the werewolves themselves, often including other paranormal beings such as vampires, witches, and fae.

This crossover deepens the world-building, allowing for a diverse cast of characters and a wide range of magical and mystical elements. It opens the door for complex alliances, rivalries, and conflicts, all of which can unexpectedly influence the romantic plotline.

A key challenge in writing in this genre is balancing the supernatural elements with developing a believable, compelling love story. The love interest or romance should be the heart of the narrative, with supernatural aspects enhancing the relationship between the characters. This balance ensures that the story remains accessible and relatable to readers, even as they are transported into a world far removed from their own.

Chapter 1

History of the Werewolf

The history of werewolves in literature is as fascinating as it is ancient, tracing back to the very dawn of storytelling itself. This journey through time reveals not just the evolution of a myth but also the shifting perceptions of mankind towards the wild, the unknown, and the otherworldly. Initially, werewolf tales were woven into the fabric of oral traditions, both as warnings against the dangers lurking in the dark and as explanations for the unexplainable. These early stories reflected humanity's deep connection with nature and its fear and reverence of its untamable aspects. The werewolf, caught between man and beast, emerged as a potent symbol of this duality, embodying the primal instincts that civilization sought to repress or control.

One of the earliest written references to werewolves comes from ancient Greece, notably in the work of Herodotus, who, in the 5th century BCE, wrote of the Neuri, a tribe he claimed transformed into wolves for a few days each year. This blend of history and myth illustrates the werewolf's presence in the collective imagination, even in antiquity, as a bridge between the human and the supernatural.

Roman literature further contributed to the werewolf lore with the tale of King Lycaon, who was transformed into a wolf by Zeus as punishment for his attempt to deceive the god. This story, preserved in Ovid's *"Metamorphoses,"* highlights the theme of transformation as a form of divine retribution, a motif that would recur throughout the werewolf's literary history. It also underscores the moralistic tone often accompanying such tales, serving as cautionary narratives about hubris and sacrilege.

The Middle Ages brought a resurgence of werewolf stories fueled by the spread of Christianity and the growing interest in the supernatural. In this era, werewolves often appeared as cursed individuals, their condition a punishment for sins or a result of witchcraft. The *"Bisclavret"* by Marie de France, a 12th-century lai, presents a more sympathetic view of the werewolf, portraying its protagonist not as a monster but as a nobleman trapped in lupine form by betrayal.

As Europe plunged into the Dark Ages, werewolf tales proliferated, reflecting the fears and anxieties of a continent riddled with war, disease, and superstition. These stories, circulated through folk tales and ecclesiastical writings, often depicted werewolves as agents of the devil, linking them to witchcraft and heresy. The werewolf became a scapegoat for society's ills, a tangible manifestation of the evil that men feared lurked in every shadow.

The witch trials that swept through Europe from the 15th to the 17th centuries further entwined the werewolf with themes of persecution and paranoia. Accusations of lycanthropy were not uncommon, and tales of werewolves often featured in the confessions extracted from the accused, either through coercion or delusion. These accounts, while horrific, provide insight into the societal fears of the time and the complex interplay between folklore, religion, and the law.

The 16th Century

During the 16th century, Europe was gripped by a fascination with werewolves fueled by superstition, religious beliefs, and a fear of the unknown. This period saw the publication of several influential texts that contributed to the proliferation of werewolf folklore and legends.

One notable example is the *"Wolfenbüttel Manuscript,"* a collection of documents from the 16th century that detailed alleged werewolf sightings and encounters. These accounts often described terrifying encounters with creatures believed to be werewolves, instilling fear and fascination in those who heard the tales.

Another significant event of the 16th century was the infamous case of the *"Werewolf of Bedburg."* In 1589, Peter Stumpp, a German farmer, was accused of being a werewolf and was subsequently executed for his alleged crimes. The case garnered widespread attention and fueled further speculation about the existence of werewolves.

During the 16th century also saw the publication of texts like *"The Discoverie of Witchcraft"* by Reginald Scot, which sought to debunk myths and superstitions surrounding witchcraft and supernatural beings, including werewolves. Despite efforts to rationalize and discredit belief in werewolves, the fear of these creatures persisted in the popular imagination.

Literature from this period often depicted werewolves as monstrous beings capable of unspeakable atrocities. Plays, ballads, and folk tales recounted stories of werewolves terrorizing villages and preying on unsuspecting victims. These narratives served as cautionary tales, warning against the dangers of succumbing to one's primal instincts.

The 16th century was a time of intense fascination and fear surrounding werewolves in Europe. Despite efforts to rationalize and debunk belief in these creatures, werewolf folklore continued to thrive, shaping the cultural landscape of the time and leaving a lasting legacy that would endure for centuries to come.

The 17th Century

During the 17th century, the cultural fascination with werewolves continued to evolve, albeit in a more nuanced manner. While earlier centuries saw the height of superstition and fear surrounding werewolves, this period shifted towards more rational and skeptical attitudes, particularly in educated circles. However, this did not entirely diminish the belief in werewolves, as they remained a potent symbol in literature and folklore.

In books, werewolves continued to be featured in various forms, albeit often in a more metaphorical or symbolic context rather than as literal creatures. Writers drew upon the rich folklore surrounding werewolves to explore themes of human nature, morality, and the conflict between civilization and the wild. While some works presented werewolves as monstrous figures embodying primal instincts, others used them as metaphors for the darker aspects of human behavior, such as violence, lust, and savagery.

The influence of earlier werewolf texts, such as *"The Book of Werewolves"* by Sabine Baring-Gould, continued to be felt during this period. These texts provided a wealth of material for writers and scholars interested in exploring the cultural significance of werewolf lore. Additionally, classical texts like Ovid's *"Metamorphoses"* remained popular sources of inspiration, with vivid depictions of shape-shifting and transformation resonating with audiences.

One notable development during this era was the emergence of werewolf-themed plays and theatrical productions—these works often combined horror, drama, and comedy elements, appealing to many audiences. Werewolves became a popular trope in the burgeoning genre of supernatural litera-ture, captivating readers with tales of mystery and suspense.

Despite the growing skepticism towards supernatural beliefs in educated circles, werewolf folklore persisted in rural and less-educated communities. Stories of alleged werewolf sightings and encounters continued circulating, perpetuating the myth of these fearsome creatures. The fear of were-wolves remained deeply ingrained in the collective psyche, serving as a reminder of humanity's primal fears and the enduring power of myth and legend.

The 18th Century

The 18th century marked a fascinating period in the folklore and literary portrayal of these enigmatic creatures. Initially, werewolf tales were steeped in superstition and fear, often linked with witchcraft and the devil in the collective imagi-nation of European societies. These early narratives primarily depicted werewolves as evil beings, cursed indi-viduals who transformed into wolves under the influence of a full moon, wreaking havoc on unsuspecting communities. The werewolf's curse was frequently seen as a punishment for sinful behavior or a sign of a pact with dark forces, reflecting the period's deep-seated fears of the unknown and the untamed aspects of nature.

As the century progressed, a subtle shift began to emerge in the portrayal of werewolves, partly influenced by the Enlightenment's emphasis on reason and a growing interest in the natural world. This era saw the first attempts to understand werewolf legends through a more scientific lens, exploring possible explanations for the myths that didn't rely solely on supernatural causes. Despite these efforts, werewolves remained largely feared figures in popular stories, symbolizing the dangers lurking beyond the edges of civilized society and the primal instincts residing within every human being.

Literature began reflecting this evolving perspective, incorporating werewolves into Gothic tales emphasizing mystery, horror, and the sublime. While not yet romantic heroes, these werewolves were often tragic figures, trapped by a fate they could not control and struggling with their dual nature. It was a period of transition, during which the seeds of sympathy for the werewolf's plight were sown, setting the stage for the more complex characterizations that would develop in the following century.

One notable example from this period is the story of Peter Stubbe, a man from Bedburg, Germany, who was accused of being a werewolf, witch, and cannibal in the late 16th century. Though his tale comes from slightly earlier, it was retold in various forms throughout the 18th century, illustrating the era's fascination with werewolf lore. As recounted in pamphlets and ballads, Stubbe's story painted him as a figure to be both feared and pitied, a victim of dark forces beyond his control. This tale, among others, reflected the complex relationship between society and the werewolf concept, embodying both the fear of the beast within and a tragic sense of inevitability.

Towards the end of the 18th century, the stage was set for a transformation in the werewolf's literary journey. The Gothic novel, with its emphasis on emotion, the past, and the supernatural, provided an ideal medium for exploring the werewolf myth in new ways. While still creatures of the night, the werewolves of this era began to acquire more depth, becoming symbols of the wild, untamed forces of nature and the dark recesses of the human psyche. This period laid the groundwork for the dramatic evolution of werewolf lore in the 19th century, where these creatures would move from the shadows of fear and superstition into the limelight of romance and heroism, forever changing how we see them.

19th Century

During the 19th century, the werewolf narrative experienced a transformation that would eventually pave the way for its inclusion in romantic fiction. This period, characterized by a rich kaleidoscope of Gothic and Romantic literature, began to explore the werewolf as a creature of horror and a being capable of complex emotions and moral dilemmas. The literature of this time played a crucial role in humanizing the werewolf, allowing for a deeper exploration of its nature and the possibilities of love and redemption amidst the curse of lycanthropy.

One significant literary work that contributed to the evolution of the werewolf myth in the 19th century was *"The Phantom Ship"* (1839) by Captain Marryat. Within this novel lies the tale of the Dog Fiend, or "The Werewolf of the Baltic," a narrative that intertwines the werewolf myth with elements of redemption and tragedy. Marryat's story provided one of the early instances where the werewolf's curse is depicted as a source of both horror and pity, highlighting the dual nature of the creature and setting the stage for the complex characters that would populate later werewolf romances.

Another pivotal work was *"Wagner the Wehr-Wolf"* (1847) by George W.M. Reynolds. This serialized novel was among the first to place a werewolf as its protagonist, exploring themes of longevity, the corrupting influence of power, and the possibility of redemption. Reynolds's portrayal of Wagner offered a nuanced look at the werewolf legend, presenting the protagonist's struggle with his curse in a sympathetic light. This narrative marked a significant departure from the purely monstrous depiction of were-wolves, suggesting that love and human connection could play a role in the werewolf's existence.

The latter part of the 19th century saw the publication of *Sabine Baring-Gould's "The Book of Were-Wolves" (1865)*, one of the first comprehensive studies on lycanthropy. While not a work of fiction, this book collected werewolf myths and legends from various cultures, examining them through historical, mythological, and anthropological lenses. Baring-Gould's work contributed to a growing public interest in werewolves, providing a wealth of material that would inspire future authors to explore the theme in novel ways, including its romantic potential.

In 1886, Clemence Housman published *"The Were-Wolf,"* a novella that further explored the conflict inherent in the werewolf's nature. Housman's story focuses on a female werewolf, a rarity in werewolf literature, who must navigate her predatory nature while maintaining human relationships. This work emphasized the tragedy of the werewolf's existence but also hinted at themes of sacrifice, love, and the possibility of redemption, which would become central to the werewolf romance genre.

As the 19th century drew to a close, the stage was set for the emergence of the werewolf romance genre. The literary works of this era began to shift the perception of werewolves from mere monsters to complex characters capable of love and heroism. This transformation was facilitated by the Romantic movement's emphasis on emotion, individualism, and the exploration of the sublime, allowing the werewolf to emerge as a figure of both fear and sympathy.

The 19th century's contribution to the werewolf narrative laid the groundwork for future explorations of the theme in literature. By the end of the century, werewolves were no longer confined to the role of antagonists or horror figures; they had become potential protagonists with stories that could encompass not just fear and tragedy but also love, redemption, and the struggle for identity. This evolution reflected broader changes in literature and society's approach to the supernatural, setting the stage for the diverse portrayals of werewolves that readers enjoy today.

It was also a transformative period for the werewolf in literature, marking the beginning of a shift from horror to romance. Through the works of Marryat, Reynolds, Housman, and others, the werewolf was gradually reimagined as a more nuanced and sympathetic character. This era sowed the seeds for the rich and varied exploration of werewolf lore in modern literature, where the themes of love, conflict, and redemption continue to resonate with readers worldwide.

20th Century

The 20th century witnessed a resurgence of interest in werewolves, driven by literature, film, and popular culture. Werewolves became iconic figures in horror fiction, with writers and filmmakers drawing upon centuries of folklore to create compelling narratives that captivated audiences worldwide. One notable example is *"The Werewolf of Paris"* by Guy Endore, published in 1933. This novel tells the story of a man who discovers he is a werewolf and explores themes of identity, sexuality, and societal repression.

The 20th century also saw the rise of werewolf-themed films, beginning with classics like *"The Wolf Man" (1941)*, starring Lon Chaney Jr. This film introduced audiences to the tragic figure of Larry Talbot, a man cursed to transform into a werewolf under the light of the full moon. "The Wolf Man" and its sequels helped popularize the werewolf genre in cinema and established many of the tropes and conventions that would define werewolf lore for decades to come.

In the latter half of the 20th century, werewolves continued to be featured prominently in literature and film. One notable example is Anne Rice's "The Wolf Gift" (2012), which reimagines the werewolf mythos in a modern setting. Rice's novel explores themes of transformation, morality, and the search for identity, appealing to readers drawn to supernatural fiction and philosophical exploration.

The 20th century also saw the emergence of werewolf-themed television shows, such as *"Buffy the Vampire*

Slayer" and *"Teen Wolf."* These series brought werewolves into the homes of millions of viewers and introduced new generations to the allure of these mythical creatures. "Buffy the Vampire Slayer," in particular, featured memorable werewolf characters like Oz, played by Seth Green, whose struggle with his lycanthropy added depth and complexity to the show's supernatural mythology.

In addition to literature and film, werewolves also found their way into other forms of popular culture, including comic books, video games, and role-playing games. For example, the *"Werewolf: The Apocalypse"* role-playing game, first published in 1992, allowed players to step into the shoes of werewolves and explore a world of supernatural conflict and intrigue.

The 20th century also saw a resurgence of interest in werewolf folklore and mythology among scholars and researchers. Academic studies and articles explored the historical roots of werewolf legends, their cultural significance, and their portrayal in literature and art. This scholarly interest helped to contextualize werewolf lore within the broader framework of folklore studies and shed new light on its enduring appeal.

Overall, the 20th century was a time of renewed interest and innovation in the portrayal of werewolves in literature, film, and popular culture. From classic novels and films to modern television shows and video games, werewolves continued to captivate audiences with their blend of horror, mystery, and tragedy. As we entered the 21st century, the legacy of the werewolf remained as potent and enduring as ever, ensuring that these mythical creatures would continue to haunt our imaginations for generations to come.

21st Century

The 21st century has seen a continuation of the fascination with werewolves, with the mythical creatures remaining a staple in literature, film, television, and popular culture. Writers and filmmakers have continued to explore the themes of transformation, identity, and primal instincts through the lens of werewolf lore, creating compelling narratives that resonate with audiences worldwide.

Werewolves have been featured in a diverse range of literature, from traditional horror novels to young adult fiction and urban fantasy. One notable example is Maggie Stiefvater's 2009 novel, *Shiver.* This novel tells the story of a teenage girl who falls in love with a boy who transforms into a werewolf, exploring themes of love, loss, and acceptance. Stiefvater's lyrical prose and nuanced characters have earned "Shiver" critical acclaim and a devoted fanbase.

The 21st century has also seen the rise of werewolf-themed television shows, with series like *"True Blood"* and *"Being Human"* exploring the complexities of werewolf identity and society. "True Blood," based on the *"Southern Vampire*

Mysteries" novels by Charlaine Harris, features a diverse cast of supernatural creatures, including werewolves, vampires, and shapeshifters. The show's exploration of werewolf politics and culture has made it a hit with fans of the genre.

Werewolves have also made their mark in American film, with standalone movies and franchise installments featuring the iconic creatures. One notable example is *"Twilight: New Moon"* (2009), the second film in the "Twilight" series based on the novels by Stephenie Meyer. In this installment, Jacob Black transforms into a werewolf, setting the stage for a love triangle between him, Bella Swan, and the vampire Edward Cullen.

The 21st century has also seen the continued popularity of werewolf-themed video games, with titles like *"The Witcher 3: Wild Hunt"* and *"The Elder Scrolls V: Skyrim"* featuring werewolf characters and storylines. These games allow players to explore immersive fantasy worlds filled with supernatural creatures, including werewolves, and experience the thrill of lycanthropic transformation firsthand.

The 21st century has seen the werewolf genre expand into various media platforms, including graphic novels and webcomics. One notable example is *"The Howling: Revenge of the Werewolf Queen,"* a graphic novel series written by Micky Neilson and illustrated by Jason Johnson, first published in 2017. This series expands upon the mythology established in the original *"The Howling"* film franchise, offering a fresh take on werewolf lore with its blend of horror, action, and supernatural intrigue.

Werewolves have also made their presence felt in the world of animation, with animated films and television series featuring werewolf characters and storylines. One notable example is the animated television series *"Teen Titans,"* which aired from 2003 to 2006. In one episode titled *"The Beast Within,"* the character of *Beast Boy* transforms into a werewolf-like creature, exploring themes of inner turmoil and self-acceptance.

There has been an emergence of werewolf-themed podcasts, with audio dramas and storytelling podcasts exploring the mysteries and horrors of lycanthropy. One notable example is *"The Black Tapes Podcast,"* a serialized supernatural thriller that features an episode titled *"The Wolves of Tesco."* *In this episode,* the hosts investigate reports of werewolf sightings in a small town in England. The episode combines horror, mystery, and suspense to create a gripping narrative that keeps listeners on the edge of their seats.

In addition, werewolves have also found a home in interactive storytelling platforms, such as alternate reality games (ARGs) and immersive theater experiences. These interactive experiences allow participants to become part of the story, engaging with characters and solving puzzles to uncover the truth behind the mystery. One notable example is *"Wolf 359,"* an ARG that challenges players to investigate a series of strange occurrences in a fictional town plagued by rumors of werewolf attacks.

Finally, the werewolf genre has also seen a resurgence of interest in werewolf mythology in non-Western cultures, with filmmakers and writers worldwide exploring their unique interpretations of lycanthropy. One notable example is the South Korean film *"A Werewolf Boy"* (2012), directed by Jo Sung-hee. The film tells the story of a young girl who befriends a feral boy with werewolf-like traits, exploring themes of friendship, love, and acceptance in a supernatural setting.

Chapter 2

What is it about Werewolves?

The charm behind werewolf characters is deeply rooted in their representation of nature's wild, untamed, and mysterious species. These creatures captivate the imagination by embodying the primal instincts and freedoms that civilization has taught humanity to suppress. With their dual existence, werewolves navigate the complexities of living both as humans and as symbols of nature's untamed spirit. This dichotomy presents a fascinating exploration of identity, allowing readers and viewers to vicariously experience the exhilaration of unleashing their hidden selves.

Werewolves often serve as metaphors for the human struggle with inner darkness and the desire for freedom. Their transformations represent the release of pent-up emotions and desires, offering a narrative space where societal norms' boundaries are crossed, and nature's raw power is embraced. This aspect of werewolf lore appeals to the longing for a connection with something greater and more elemental than the structured confines of modern life. The lure lies in the liberation from human limitations, tapping into the collective unconscious that yearns to return to the wild.

Moreover, their mysterious nature adds to their intrigue. The transformation from human to wolf, often shrouded in secrecy and magic, invites intrigue and fascination. This mystery extends to their origins, behaviors, and the lore surrounding them, which varies widely across cultures and stories. The unknown elements of werewolf mythology spark curiosity and invite audiences to delve deeper into the supernatural world, seeking to understand the forces that drive these creatures.

The wildness of the werewolf species also resonates with audiences through its embodiment of natural instincts and purity. Unlike humans, who are often seen as disconnected from the natural world, werewolves operate on instinct, free from societal constructs and moral dilemmas. This portrayal of werewolves as beings of pure emotion and action strikes a chord with those who feel burdened by the complexities of human society. The intrigue here lies in the simplicity of their existence, which contrasts sharply with the often overwhelming nature of human life.

Romantic portrayals of these wild creatures have further amplified their fascination. Their fierce loyalty, protective instincts, and capacity for deep, passionate love present a compelling picture of primal romance in these narratives. The intensity of their relationships, often marked by themes of fated mates and eternal bonds, speaks to the desire for a love that transcends the ordinary, offering an escape into a world where love is as wild and untamed as the creatures themselves.

The lure of werewolves is also found in their representation as symbols of rebellion and resistance. Their refusal to conform to human or supernatural laws mirrors the rebellious spirit in many, celebrating the courage to stand apart and live by one's own rules. This aspect fascinates the part of us that rebels against conformity, admiring characters who embody strength, independence, and defiance in the face of adversity.

Furthermore, their characters challenge our understanding of humanity and morality. Through their struggles with their dual nature, werewolves pose questions about what it means to be human and the nature of the beast within us all. This exploration of moral gray areas and the potential for savagery and compassion within each person adds depth to werewolf narratives, engaging audiences in philosophical contemplation.

Their portrayal as protectors of their packs and territories taps into the human instinct to protect one's family and home. This depiction of loyalty and sacrifice resonates deeply, illustrating the value of community and belonging. It highlights the idea that strength comes from unity and that even those who live on the fringes of society have their own forms of honor and duty.

They embody the theme of transformation, both literal and metaphorical. Their ability to change shape reflects the human capacity for change and growth, serving as a powerful metaphor for personal development and self-discovery. This aspect of werewolf lore appeals to the universal human experience of undergoing significant life changes, emphasizing the potential for rebirth and new beginnings.

In addition to their symbolic meanings, a werewolf's physical abilities—such as enhanced strength, speed, and heightened senses—offer an escape into a world where physical limitations are overcome. This trait satisfies the human fascination with power and the ability to transcend ordinary human capabilities, appealing to our instincts for adventure and exploration.

The cultural significance of werewolves adds another layer to why people are so fascinated by them. Drawing from a collage of folklore and legend, these animalist characters are imbued with the weight of centuries of storytelling. This historical and cultural depth deepens the wolf's narratives, connecting them to a broader human experience and inviting audiences to explore diverse traditions and interpretations of myth.

The evolution of werewolves in film and literature reflects changing societal attitudes towards nature, freedom, and the unknown. As these narratives have shifted from horror to romance and urban fantasy, the werewolf has become a versatile symbol for exploring *the wild side*. This adaptability grants werewolf characters' continued relevance and lore, allowing them to resonate with new generations of wolfy fans to come.

Chapter 3

It's All About the Lore

In the dark moonlit nights of werewolf romances, the creatures that stalk the night are not mere monsters but beings of complex lore and intricate characteristics. To breathe life into your werewolves is to delve deep into the ancient woods of myth and emerge with a terrifying and mesmerizing creature. This chapter will guide you through the forest of creation, where every howl in the dark is a tale waiting to be told, and every set of glowing eyes a character waiting to be understood. The first step in this creative process is establishing the origins of your werewolves. Are they descendants of ancient gods, cursed by evil forces, or the result of an evolutionary twist? For example, in *The Mercy Thompson Series,* Patricia Briggs introduces werewolves as beings who coexist with humans, each with a unique origin story that ties into the broader lore of the supernatural world.

The genesis of your werewolves begins with their lore, the bedrock upon which all else is built. Across cultures, werewolves have been feared and revered, seen as both gods and demons. In crafting your own, consider the tangle of myths at your disposal. From the cursed wolves of Eastern Europe, bound by blood and moon, to the skinwalkers of Native American tradition, where transformation is a gift of the spirits, your lore should be a blend of the ancient and the personal. Your werewolves could be the descendants of Lycaon, cursed by Zeus for his hubris, or perhaps they are warriors chosen by the moon to protect their lands, as in the *"Mercy Thompson"* series.

Consider the nature of transformation. Is it a curse, an inherited trait, or a chosen path? The physical transformation from human to wolf is a spectacle of horror and beauty, a dance of bone and ligament that should be described with reverence for the pain and the power it bestows. In *"Bitten"* by Kelley Armstrong, transformation is a genetic trait passed down and triggered by emotional stress or the pull of the full moon. The detail with which Armstrong describes the process—the tearing of clothes, the reshaping of limbs, the mix of agony and euphoria—serves to ground the supernatural in the visceral reality of the body.

But what of the wolf itself? The true heart of your werewolf lies in its dual nature. The wolf is not just a beast but a symbol of the wild, untamed, and free. Its characteristics—

pack loyalty, territorialism, predatory instinct—should mirror and magnify the human personality of your werewolf. A lone wolf character might struggle with isolation and the longing for connection, while an Alpha might grapple with the weight of leadership and the responsibility to protect. In Nalini Singh's *"Psy/Changeling"* series, the Changelings are portrayed with a depth of emotion and complexity that showcases the interplay between their animal instincts and their human desires.

Communication is another facet where your werewolves' duality can shine. The ability to speak in human and wolf forms or through mind links, as seen in many paranormal romances, adds a layer of connection and mystery. How your werewolves communicate within the pack and with others can reveal much about their society and their place within it. The mind link, a common trope, facilitates instant communication and serves as a symbol of the deep bonds that unite the pack, transcending physical distance and circumstance.

Traditions within werewolf lore serve as the backbone of your society, offering a glimpse into the collective psyche of your creatures. Consider the significance of the full moon, a common element in werewolf mythology. How do your werewolves respond to it? Is it a time of power or vulnerability? Kelley Armstrong's *Women of the Otherworld* series showcases diverse traditions among supernatural beings, including werewolves, emphasizing how these rituals shape their identities and relationships.

The powers you bestow upon your werewolves can range from the classic enhanced strength and speed to more unique abilities tailored to fit the world you're building. It's crucial, however, to establish limitations to these powers to maintain tension and stakes within your story. For instance, Charlaine Harris's *Sookie Stackhouse* novels feature werewolves with rooted strengths but also vulnerabilities that play a significant role in the narrative, reminding us that power often comes with a price. You can include powers of enhanced strength, speed, heightened senses, and rapid healing. However, consider adding unique abilities that fit your world, such as control over natural elements, psychic communication, or shapeshifting at will, not just under the full moon. Balancing these powers with limitations—such as vulnerability to silver, uncontrollable shifts during emotional turmoil, or a weakened state after transforming— can add depth and tension to your story.

Limitations are essential to werewolf lore, preventing your characters from becoming too powerful and ensuring they remain relatable. These can be physical, such as the painful transformation process or a dependency on the moon's cycles. They might also be societal, like laws that govern werewolf behavior in human society or taboos within the werewolf community. Limitations add complexity to your characters' lives and drive plot development, forcing were-wolves to navigate their world carefully and creatively.

Societal structure is another key aspect of the lore. Most werewolf societies are depicted as hierarchical, but the nature of this hierarchy can vary significantly. In *The Twilight* Saga by Stephenie Meyer, werewolves live in a tight-knit pack led by an alpha, but their relationships with vampires and humans deeply influence their structure. This inter-species dynamic adds layers to the societal structure, creating a complex web of alliances and conflicts. Most werewolf societies are depicted as organized into packs with a strict chain of command. The alpha is typically at the top, serving as the leader and protector of the pack. Below the alpha, there might be a beta, the alpha's second-in-command and enforcer, and omegas, who occupy the lowest rung of the hierarchy. This structure can influence every aspect of werewolf life, from decision-making processes to interper-sonal relationships within the pack.

Consider how your werewolves interact with the human world. Do they live in secrecy, hidden from human eyes, or are they known and integrated into human society? This choice can significantly impact your story, affecting every-thing from the setting to your characters' conflicts. A hidden society might struggle with issues of isolation and identity, while a known society could face prejudice and integration challenges.

Becoming a werewolf is another facet of your lore to define. Is lycanthropy inherited, passed down through generations, or is it transmitted through bites or scratches? The method of transmission can influence werewolf culture and individual identities. Inherited lycanthropy might come with family expectations and legacies, while transmission through bites could introduce themes of change, loss, and acceptance.

Conflict within the lore often arises from the tension between the werewolf's dual nature. Exploring how your werewolves reconcile their human desires with their animal instincts can provide a rich vein of character development and plot progression. This internal conflict can be mirrored in external struggles, such as disputes between packs, challenges to leadership, or confrontations with humans or other supernatural beings.

Rituals and ceremonies can deepen the cultural aspect of your werewolf's society, marking important events such as the first transformation, the full moon, or the changing of alphas. These rituals can be moments of community bonding, conflict, or both, offering a glimpse into your werewolves' spiritual and emotional well-being. They can also serve as plot points, providing a setting for crucial developments or revelations.

The lore-surrounding werewolf transformations are fertile ground for creativity. Consider the triggers (emotional stress, the full moon), the experience (painful, euphoric), and the aftermath (memory loss, exhaustion). These details can make your werewolves' experiences more vivid and their struggles poignant, affecting their relationships, goals, and sense of self.

Integration with other supernatural beings can add layers to your lore. Whether werewolves exist in a world with vampires, witches, or other creatures can shape their societal structure, traditions, and conflicts. This integration can create alliances, rivalries, and complex social dynamics that adds to your narrative landscape.

Environmental themes can also be woven into your lore, reflecting the creatures' connection to the natural world. Their territories, the sacredness of the land, and conflicts over human encroachment can all play significant roles in your narrative, similar to themes explored in *The Last Werewolf* by Glen Duncan.

The moral and ethical dilemmas inherent in being a creature of dual nature offer rich narrative potential. The struggle with the beast within, the fear of losing control, and the quest for redemption are themes that resonate deeply. Your werewolves are not just predators but beings caught between two worlds, seeking balance. This internal conflict can drive your narrative, providing a compelling counterpoint to your characters' external challenges.

Lastly, the sensory world of your werewolf is a canvas only you can paint. The rush of scents on the wind, the spectrum of colors at night, and the sounds of the forest are amplified —these details immerse your reader in the werewolf's experience. The world through the eyes of the wolf is a place of heightened awareness, where every leaf rustle tells a story, and every scent carries a message.

Chapter 4

Setting the Scene

Diving into the world of werewolves, the setting isn't just a backdrop; it's a vital piece of the story that wraps around characters and plot, shaping and defining them. To truly bring your werewolf romance to life, you must construct a world that feels as real and vibrant as the characters. This chapter will guide you through creating a setting that breathes, loves, and growls with the heart of your story.

Begin with the wilderness—the deep, dark forests where the moon casts long shadows between the trees and the werewolf's howl echoes through the night. This primeval landscape is the heartland of your werewolf lore, where the wild reigns supreme. In the untamed woods, it's here that your characters will find their true selves, challenged by the elements and each other. The wilderness serves as a metaphor for the untamed nature of the werewolf, reflecting their primal instincts and desires. Consider the dense forests of the Pacific Northwest, a popular setting for werewolf tales, where the thick fog and endless rain add a layer of mystery and isolation.

But the setting of your story extends beyond the physical environment to the communities that inhabit it. Small, secluded towns on the edge of the wilderness offer a unique blend of intimacy and secrecy. These towns provide fertile ground for your narrative with their close-knit communities and generations-old secrets. They are places where the human and the supernatural collide, where the werewolves can hide in plain sight. The dynamic between the townsfolk and the werewolves adds complexity to the setting, creating a tension that simmers beneath the surface of everyday life.

The architecture and design of the spaces your characters inhabit also play a crucial role in setting the scene. The ancestral home of a werewolf pack, with its hidden rooms and ancient artifacts, tells a story of heritage and power. These homes are not just places of refuge but symbols of the pack's identity and strength. They hold the history of the pack within their walls, from the portraits of Alpha leaders past to the sacred spaces where rituals are performed. Every stone and beam is imbued with the essence of the pack, a testament to their survival and sovereignty.

Night plays a unique role in werewolf romances, transforming the familiar into the unknown and the safe into the dangerous. The shift from day to night alters the mood of the setting, cloaking the world in mystery and potential. The night is a time of freedom and transformation, where the werewolves can roam unbound by their human guise. It's a time of magic, where the veil between the worlds thins, and the supernatural feels closer, more tangible. The way the moonlight filters through the trees, the silence that envelops the world, the sudden rustle that signifies the presence of something unseen—all these elements contribute to the atmosphere of your setting, enhancing the sense of mystery and anticipation.

Contrastingly, the urban landscape offers a different stage for your werewolf romance. The bustling city, with its neon lights and crowded streets, might seem anathema to the werewolf's nature, but it, too, can be a rich setting. The contrast between the wolf's wild instincts and the constraints of the urban environment creates a tension that can drive the narrative. The city becomes a jungle of concrete and steel, where the werewolves must navigate a different kind of wilderness. The juxtaposition of their dual identities—human by day, werewolf by night—plays out against the backdrop of the city's chaos, reflecting the inner turmoil of your characters.

The changing seasons provide another layer to your setting, marking the passage of time and influencing the story's mood. The stark beauty of winter, with its blanket of snow and biting cold, can mirror the isolation or purity of love.

With its renewal and growth, spring might symbolize new beginnings or the rekindling of old flames. Each season carries its symbolism and palette of colors and emotions, which can enhance the narrative and deepen the reader's connection to the story.

Building a world where the supernatural coexists with the ordinary is a delicate balancing act. Your setting should be where extraordinary creatures move in the shadows of the everyday world, where magic is felt if not always seen. This blending of the mundane and the magical creates a rich, immersive experience, drawing readers deeper into the story.

The essence of an excellent werewolf romance setting lies in its ability to put the readers in place, making them feel the chill of the night air, the tension of a hunt, or the warmth of a pack gathered in solidarity. By building a detailed, dynamic, and deeply interwoven world with your characters' lives, you create a setting that is not just a place but a living part of your story.

Remember, the setting of your story is more than just geographical; it's the heartbeat of your narrative, a character in its own right that evolves, challenges, and perfects your story. Whether your characters prowl through shadowed forests, navigate the complexities of small-town life, or hunt in the concrete jungle, their environment should pulse with life, echoing the wild call of the werewolf.

In crafting your scene, we do more than create a setting; we forge a world alive with passion and struggle. It's a domain where the raw essence of the werewolves meets the enduring strength of love, refining every element of the setting with the story's vibrant threads. In the heart of the wild and mysterious, our characters discover not only each other but their true selves, with their love shining as a guiding light through the darkness.

As the moon charts its course through the heavens, the scene is set, ready for a tale of desire, change, and the timeless dance between shadow and illumination. In this world, love is the greatest adventure, inviting us into the depths of the heart, a place ventured only by the courageous.

Chapter 5

The Romantic Arc

Writing a love story set in the world of werewolves involves a careful mix of passion, tension, and change. The story leads readers on a journey that not only draws them closer to the characters but also showcases the growth each character undergoes against a backdrop filled with supernatural challenges.

The journey of love often starts with a spark—an unexpected meeting or a pivotal event that draws the protagonists into each other's lives. This initial connection might be fraught with conflict, curiosity, or an unexplainable attraction, setting the stage for their chemistry to develop. In Patricia Briggs' *Moon Called*, for example, Mercy Thompson finds her life entwined with that of the werewolves not through immediate allure but through deep, complex bonds formed from necessity and shared experiences.

As the narrative unfolds, the characters find themselves drawn closer by experiences that test their mettle and reveal their true selves. This phase is dotted with moments where they see past each other's facades, recognizing the soul underneath. Kelley Armstrong's *Bitten* paints a vivid picture of this, showing Elena Michaels and Clayton Danvers wrestling with their turbulent past and the stark realities of their werewolf existence, their connection deepening through mutual understanding and acceptance.

The story intensifies when challenges emerge, putting the budding relationship to the test. These hurdles can come from outside forces like rival packs or hunters or from within as they grapple with accepting their bond. The tension between desire and obligation is portrayed compellingly in *Alpha & Omega* by Patricia Briggs, where Charles and Anna navigate their duties to their pack while exploring the growing trust and fondness between them.

A critical turning point is recognizing their bond or realizing deep-seated emotions, often occurring when they least expect it but most need hope. In *The Mating* by Nicky Charles, acknowledging the mate bond brings not only the promise of love but also a host of responsibilities and dangers, underscoring the significance of such a connection in their society.

As the stakes rise with escalating conflict, the protagonists face the reality of their relationship and the potential sacrifices it entails. Their fight for survival, acceptance, and the freedom to love adds layers to their romance, making their journey all the more gripping. Nalini Singh's *Psy-Changeling* series masterfully explores these themes, entwining politics, power, and passion in a way that challenges the characters' loyalties and loves.

Intimacy—physical and emotional—throughout the story offers a window into the evolving relationship, highlighting the growing trust and understanding between the characters. In *The Phoenix Pack* series by Suzanne Wright, such moments mark significant milestones in their relationship, each deepening their connection and solidifying their bond.

The climax often aligns with a decisive confrontation or revelation, forcing the characters to choose their love over daunting obstacles. This peak isn't just about resolving the immediate conflict but affirming their commitment to each other. *The Wolves of Mercy Falls* series by Maggie Stiefvater showcases this beautifully, with Sam and Grace facing supernatural and human hurdles to remain together.

Following the climax, a new balance is found where the protagonists, now stronger and more united, face the future together. This resolution doesn't imply a perfect ending but acknowledges their love and the ongoing challenges they'll confront together. *Moon Called* sees Mercy and Adam tackling their bond with an awareness of its strength and the resilience it adds to their lives.

The narrative might also explore how their love alters their position within their community, showing how their relationship affects their social roles. This exploration highlights the transformative power of love, how it reshapes their lives and the world around them for the better.

Secondary characters and side stories boost the main tale, adding complexity and depth to exploring love and relationships within the supernatural framework.

Humor and tender moments provide relief from the tension and conflict, underscoring that love is not only about passion and struggle but also joy, laughter, and the simple moments that build a life together.

The setting mirrors and amplifies the love story, with wild landscapes reflecting the raw and intense nature of werewolf love. Whether it's a forest, a pack territory, or a secluded spot, each location is laden with symbolism.

Themes of fate versus free will often intertwine through werewolf romances. The mate bond is a central element in this exploration, adding depth to their choice and commitment to each other.

The portrayal of werewolf nature, embodying primal instincts and the struggle for control, mirrors the tumultuous path of love, showcasing the characters' complexities and the acceptance they find in each other.

In the end, a glimpse into the future through an epilogue celebrates their enduring love, a testament to the strength and permanence of their bond, inspiring others in their world.

Focusing on these elements can create a romance that deeply resonates with readers of the werewolf genre.

Chapter 6

Balancing Act Between Real and Supernatural

Balancing the real and the supernatural in a werewolf romance story is a knotty dance requiring a careful blend of everyday life and the magical, creating a world that feels both tangible and enchanted. The key to this balance lies in grounding the supernatural elements within the familiar framework of human emotions, desires, and conflicts. This approach allows readers to relate to the characters and their struggles, even navigating a world filled with werewolves, ancient rituals, and other fantastical elements.

Establishing clear rules for your supernatural world is key. These rules provide a framework that lends consistency and believability to the fantastical aspects of your story. For instance, detailing the mechanics of werewolf transformation—the triggers, limitations, and physical effects—help readers suspend disbelief and engage with the narrative.

Setting these parameters creates stakes and challenges for your characters, grounding the supernatural in a reality that readers can understand and anticipate.

Another important strategy is seamlessly integrating the supernatural into the everyday world. This can be achieved by placing supernatural events and elements in familiar settings—a moonlit forest where the local werewolves gather, a bustling city where they hide in plain sight, or a small town with hidden depths and secrets. By blending the magical into the mundane, you create a world that feels expansive and immersive, inviting readers to explore the unknown through the safety of the known.

Character development plays a significant role in balancing the real and the supernatural. Your characters, whether human, werewolf or somewhere in between, should exhibit a range of human emotions and experiences. Their supernatural abilities or identities add layers to their character but do not overshadow their humanity. Through their eyes, the extraordinary becomes relatable. Their fears, hopes, loves, and losses become the emotional touchstones that guide readers through the fantastical aspects of your story.

Sensory details are another effective tool in making the supernatural feel tangible. Describing the texture of fur during a transformation, the scent marking a territory, or the sound of a howl echoing through the night brings the fantasy elements to life. These details bridge the gap between the reader's world and the world of the werewolves, making the supernatural experiences feel as real as any human experience.

Incorporating folklore and mythology can also enhance the believability of your supernatural world. Drawing on existing myths and legends about werewolves and other creatures provides a foundation of familiarity, tapping into your readers' collective unconscious. This polishes your storyline and anchors the fantastical elements in a broader cultural context, lending them an air of authenticity.

Contrasting the supernatural with the real highlights the impact of the fantastical on the norm. Show how the presence of werewolves affects the dynamics of a small town, alters the landscape of a city, or shifts the balance of power in a community. This contrast emphasizes the extraordinary within the ordinary and explores the consequences of the supernatural in a realistic setting.

The emotional and psychological impact of the supernatural on your characters offers another way to portray your character. How does being a werewolf affect one's sense of identity, relationships, or worldview? Delving into these questions provides depth to your characters and makes their supernatural experiences resonate with readers on a human level.

The interplay between magic and technological advancements in your world can also offer a unique blend of the real and the supernatural. How do werewolves navigate a world of smartphones, surveillance, and social media in a modern setting? This intersection between the ancient and the contemporary adds a layer of complexity to your story, making the supernatural elements feel integrated into the characters' daily lives.

Creating a history for your supernatural world that parallels our own can add depth and realism. Historical events might have supernatural causes, and famous figures could be werewolves in disguise. This blending of history and fantasy suggests that the paranormal has always been a part of the human experience, making your world feel lived-in and authentic.

Another aspect to consider is the role of the supernatural in society. How do humans perceive werewolves? Are they a secret, hidden from the wider world, or a known part of society? The interaction between the supernatural and societal norms creates a dynamic setting that reflects real-world issues of acceptance, prejudice, and integration.

Building a community around your supernatural characters, complete with its own culture, traditions, and hierarchies, helps ground the fantastical in the social realities of your world. This community provides a backdrop against which personal dramas and romances can unfold, highlighting the universality of social bonds, whether human or supernatural.

Including supernatural elements should serve the story, enhancing the plot and character development rather than overshadowing them. Each fantastical aspect should be woven into the narrative in an organic and essential way, driving the story forward and deepening the reader's engagement.

Finally, maintaining a sense of wonder and mystery is crucial. Even as you ground the supernatural in reality, preserve the magic and awe that surrounds the fantastical. This sense of wonder captivates readers, drawing them deeper into your world, where the real and the supernatural dance together in the moonlight, creating a story that is both enchanting and profoundly human.

Balancing the real and the supernatural in a werewolf romance requires a nuanced approach that respects the rules of your created world while exploring the depths of human emotion. By stitching together the fantastical and the mundane, you make a rich, immersive experience that resonates with readers, inviting them into a world where love transcends the boundaries of the ordinary.

Chapter 7

Creating your Werewolf Protagonist

Creating compelling protagonists in a werewolf romance story involves balancing human and werewolf traits. This balance adds depth to the characters and makes them more relatable to readers who navigate their own dualities in daily life. A well-drawn protagonist in this genre embodies the conflict and harmony between their human nature and supernatural identity, offering a unique perspective on the universal themes of identity, belonging, and transformation.

In the *"Alpha & Omega"* series by Patricia Briggs, Charles Cornick is an excellent example of a protagonist who embodies the balance between human logic and werewolf instincts. Charles is an enforcer for his father, the Marrok, which requires him to rely on his werewolf strength and aggression. However, his role also demands a keen understanding of human and werewolf politics, diplomacy, and empathy. Briggs crafts Charles as a character who uses his human intelligence and emotional depth to navigate the complex social structures of the werewolf world, making him a deeply layered character who resonates with readers on multiple levels.

Another compelling protagonist is Calla Tor from *"Nightshade"* by Andrea Cremer. Calla, as the alpha female of her pack, is expected to lead with strength and uphold the werewolf traditions. Yet, her human side craves the freedom to choose, especially regarding love and loyalty. Cremer skillfully depicts Calla's internal struggle as she juggles her duties to her pack with her desires as a human being. This duality adds a rich layer of conflict and character development, making Calla's journey a captivating blend of supernatural adventure and personal growth.

In *"The Wolf's Call"* by Anthony Ryan, Vaelin Al Sorna is not a werewolf but embodies a similar blend of human and 'other' that parallels the werewolf experience. His honed skills as a warrior and a heightened sense of intuition, which borders on the supernatural, set him apart from others. Ryan's depiction of Vaelin's struggle with his identity and destiny and his very human emotions and relationships serve as a masterclass in blending extraordinary abilities with relatable human qualities. This balance keeps readers invested in Vaelin's story, deeply rooting for his successes and feeling his losses.

"Moon Called," the first book in the *"Mercy Thompson"* series by Patricia Briggs, presents Mercy Thompson, a coyote shifter living among werewolves. Mercy's navigation of life reflects the tightrope walk between her human upbringing and her coyote-shapeshifter nature. Her ability to shift forms at will contrasts with the werewolves' compulsion to transform at the full moon, highlighting her unique position in the supernatural community. Mercy's independence, humor, and compassion in dealing with humans and supernatural beings create a multi-dimensional character who embodies the balance between two worlds.

"Shiver" by Maggie Stiefvater introduces us to Sam Roth, a young man who turns into a wolf each winter. Sam's struggle is profoundly human - his fight against time and fate to stay with the girl he loves, Grace, as his uncontrollable transformations loom over their relationship. Stiefvater explores the pain of separation, the fear of losing oneself, and the desperate cling to humanity through Sam, making his werewolf condition a poignant metaphor for the universal experiences of change, loss, and love.

* * *

So, first, begin with the human aspect of your protagonists. These are the traits that ground them in reality and connect them with readers on an emotional level. Human traits such as empathy, fear, love, ambition, and the quest for identity are universal experiences. For instance, Elena Michaels from Kelley Armstrong's *"Bitten"* struggles with her desire for an everyday life that is against her nature as a werewolf. Her journey of acceptance and self-discovery is relatable to readers who have experienced similar conflicts between societal expectations and personal truth.

Next, integrate the werewolf traits that set your protagonists apart and introduce the fantastical element that attracts readers to the genre. Strength, heightened senses, a deep connection to nature, and the instinctual pull of the pack are characteristics that offer a contrast to their human side. These traits can create internal conflicts, such as the struggle between the protagonist's animalistic impulses and their human moral compass. In Patricia Briggs' *"Mercy Thompson"* series, Mercy navigates her life with the heightened senses and physical prowess of a coyote shifter, alongside her human intelligence and emotions, blending her dual identities seamlessly.

The protagonists' werewolf traits should also impact their relationships, providing a rich vein of conflict and growth. The pack dynamics, emphasizing loyalty, hierarchy, and territoriality, can clash with human notions of individuality and freedom. This tension can drive the narrative and character development, as seen in Nalini Singh's *"Psy/Changeling"* series, where the changeling characters must balance their animal instincts with their deep, emotional connections to their mates and packs, highlighting the complexity of their dual natures.

To create depth and relatability, show how your protagonists' dual identities affect their view of the world and their place in it. They live in two worlds, often feeling like outsiders in both. This duality can be a source of strength, giving them a unique perspective and abilities, but it can also be a source of vulnerability and isolation. The struggle to reconcile these aspects of their identity can make for a compelling narrative as characters seek acceptance and a sense of belonging.

Incorporate moments where your protagonists' human and werewolf traits clash and merge, offering insights into their characters. For example, their werewolf strength and aggression might emerge in moments of human vulnerability or emotional distress, complicating their reactions and relationships. These moments reveal your characters' multifaceted nature, making them more complex and engaging.

Balance is key in ensuring that neither the human nor the werewolf side dominates to the detriment of character development. This balance allows for growth and change as protagonists learn to integrate their dual natures. The journey towards this integration can form the backbone of your narrative, providing a compelling arc of self-discovery and acceptance.

Utilize secondary characters and antagonists to highlight and challenge the protagonists' dual identities. The interactions with these characters can mirror the protagonists' struggles and achievements in balancing their human and werewolf traits. For example, a purely human antagonist might underestimate the protagonist's strength due to their human appearance, while a werewolf antagonist might challenge their loyalty or control.

The setting and plot should also reflect and accommodate the protagonists' dual nature. Whether it's the wild, untamed forests that call to their werewolf side or the human cities where they forge their lives and relationships, the environment plays a crucial role in shaping their identity. The challenges they face, from supernatural threats to personal dilemmas, should test their human and werewolf traits, compelling them to grow and adapt.

The most compelling protagonists in werewolf romance are those who embrace their complexity, finding power in their duality. By the end of their journey, they no longer see their human and werewolf traits as conflicting forces but as integral parts of their identity. This message of acceptance and unity resonates with readers, offering a satisfying conclusion to the protagonist's quest for self-discovery.

Through careful development and balancing of human and werewolf traits, you can create protagonists who are not only compelling but deeply relatable. Their struggles and triumphs echo the human experience, making them unforgettable characters who capture readers' hearts.

Chapter 8

Creating your Antagonist(s)

As we delve into the shadowy world of villains and bad guys/gals in the werewolf romance genre, we must recognize their pivotal role in crafting a compelling narrative. Often cloaked in darkness, these characters are not mere obstacles but catalysts for growth, pushing our heroes to their limits and beyond. Their motivations, dark reflections of our protagonists' desires, serve as a mirror to the complexities of human (and werewolf) nature. In this chapter, let's explore how to create antagonists that enhance conflict and plot progression and add depth to our storytelling.

First and foremost, a memorable antagonist in a werewolf romance needs clear, understandable motives. Take, for example, Lucien from *"The Mating"* by Nicky Charles. Lucien's quest for power and dominance over the pack is driven by a deep-seated belief in his right to lead, twisted by jealousy and a sense of betrayal. This personal vendetta against the protagonists adds a layer of intensity to the narrative, making the conflict deeply personal. By grounding Lucien's actions in relatable emotions, Charles crafts an antagonist who is not just a villain but a character with a tragic trajectory.

Another layer to consider is the antagonist's relationship with the protagonist. In *"Alpha's Claim"* by Addison Cain, Shepherd's obsession with Claire is a dark mirror to the protective love of a typical werewolf mate bond. This obsession fuels the plot and tests the limits of Claire's resilience and independence, challenging her to fight for her freedom and the love she truly desires. The dynamic between Shepherd and Claire elevates the narrative, transforming the story into a battle of wills that captivates readers.

An effective antagonist often embodies the darker aspects of the world you've created. In *"Red Moon Rising"* by Peter Moore, the societal rift between humans and werewolves is personified in the character of Sebastian, whose actions stem from a deeply ingrained prejudice. Sebastian's antagonism is a commentary on fear, hatred, and misunderstanding between different communities. His character brings to light the broader conflicts within the world, making the personal struggles of the protagonists emblematic of a larger battle for acceptance and peace.

Antagonists with complex backgrounds add richness to the story. Consider creating a villain who was once a friend or ally to the protagonist, adding a layer of betrayal to the narrative. This backstory makes the antagonist more multi-dimensional and introduces moral ambiguity, challenging readers to question what led them down a darker path. The betrayal of a once-loyal friend or family member can test the protagonist's faith in themselves and others, driving character development and plot progression.

Introducing a secondary antagonist can complicate the plot and provide additional layers of conflict. This character might not be evil in the traditional sense but could represent a rival love interest, a well-meaning but misguided authority figure, or a competing alpha. Their goals and actions can inadvertently or deliberately hinder the protagonist's progress, making the journey to the story's resolution more challenging and engaging.

Utilizing the antagonist's perspective can offer readers insight into their motivations and provide a richer narrative experience. Brief chapters or sections from the antagonist's point of view can illuminate their reasoning and humanize them, adding depth to the story. This technique allows readers to engage with the antagonist on a more personal level, understanding the complexities of their character beyond their role as a mere obstacle.

The environment or society can act as an antagonist, presenting challenges stemming from the world's inherent dangers or prejudices. In such narratives, the protagonists must navigate a hostile or indifferent landscape to their struggles, reflecting themes of survival, resilience, and the fight for justice. This broader conflict can underscore the personal battles faced by the characters, highlighting their bravery and determination.

Crafting an antagonist with a personal connection to the protagonist amplifies the emotional stakes of the conflict. A family member turned rival, a betrayed friend or a former lover can provide a compelling backstory and a deeper emotional resonance to the narrative. The personal history between the protagonist and antagonist reinforces the conflict, making it more than just a battle of strength but a clash of hearts and histories.

The antagonist's downfall or redemption is a pivotal moment in the narrative. Whether they face consequences for their actions or find a path to redemption, this arc should feel earned and reflective of the story's themes. The resolution of the antagonist's journey can offer closure, catharsis, or even a glimmer of hope, reinforcing the story's message and the growth of its characters.

Remember, the strength of your antagonist lies in their ability to challenge your protagonist in meaningful ways. They should force your heroes to confront their fears, question their beliefs, and ultimately grow stronger. The conflict sparked by the antagonist propels the story forward, blending tension and excitement through the narrative.

In crafting your werewolf romance, your antagonists are as crucial as your heroes. They are the storm that tests the strength of your protagonists, the shadow that makes the light shine brighter. By creating villains and antagonists with depth, motivation, and complexity, you deepen your narrative, engaging your readers with a story that resonates with the truth of the human (and werewolf) experience.

Chapter 9

Make your Characters Likeable

The characters you create are the heart and soul of your story. Their journeys, struggles, and triumphs will captivate readers from the first page to the last. Crafting strong, likable characters—human and werewolf—is crucial to inscribing a narrative that resonates deeply with your audience. This chapter will guide you through the intricacies of building characters that leap off the page, drawing from the traits inherent to both their human and werewolf natures.

As you take on writing a story in this genre, remember that your characters are the windows through which readers experience your world. Strong characters are not merely powerful in the physical sense; they possess depth, resilience, and the capacity to grow. Likability, on the other hand, does not mean that your characters must be flawless. Instead, it's their relatability, their struggles, and their moral compass that endear them to readers. Let's explore how to blend human and werewolf traits to create complex characters who can carry the weight of your story.

It's pivotal to delve deep into the embodiment of traits that render your protagonists compelling and relatable. The balance between their human and werewolf identities refines their characterization and enhances the readers' engagement and empathy towards them. Let's look at some examples:

The character of Derek Hale from the television series *"Teen Wolf."* Derek's journey encapsulates the tumultuous path of embracing his werewolf heritage while grappling with his human emotions and moral compass. His character arc is a testament to resilience, showcasing how personal loss and betrayal shape his actions and decisions. Derek's struggle for redemption and protecting those he cares about endears him to the audience, illustrating the impact of well-rounded character development.

In *"The Grey Wolves Series"* by Quinn Loftis, the character of Jacque Pierce offers an engaging look at a protagonist who finds herself thrust into the werewolf world. Jacque's humor, loyalty, and strength in the face of a new and often terrifying reality endear her to readers. Her journey of discovering love with a werewolf prince and navigating the intricacies of pack dynamics highlights her resilience and adaptability, which resonate deeply with those who face challenges in adapting to new situations.

"Prince of Wolves," the first book in the series, sets the stage for Jacque's evolution from a typical high school student to a central figure in a werewolf pack, illustrating the power of love and friendship in overcoming adversity. Her likability stems from her genuine reactions, witty banter, and the depth of her emotions, making her a relatable and compelling figure.

Ilona Andrews' *"Kate Daniels Series"* introduces readers to a dynamic world where magic and the supernatural are commonplace. While Kate Daniels is not a werewolf, her interactions with shapeshifters and other supernatural beings and her own magical heritage create a rich collage of experiences that echo the dual nature of werewolf protagonists. Kate's fierce independence, sharp wit, and unwavering commitment to protecting those she cares about make her a standout character in urban fantasy and paranormal romance. Her relationship with Curran, the Beast Lord, is particularly notable for its exploration of power dynamics, trust, and adaptation, which is central to the werewolf romance genre.

"The Phoenix Pack Series" by Suzanne Wright showcases a variety of likable characters, each with unique challenges and strengths. Characters like Taryn Warner, a latent shifter, and Trey Coleman, an alpha male with a tumul-

tuous past, exemplify the balance between vulnerability and strength. Their romance, fraught with external pressures and internal fears, showcases the importance of acceptance and the power of love to transcend differences. Wright excels in creating characters whose personal growth and relationships are as compelling as their supernatural escapades, making the series a beloved staple in the genre.

"Moon Called," the first book in Patricia Briggs' "Mercy Thompson Series," brings another dimension to likable characters in werewolf romance through the protagonist, Mercy Thompson. A mechanic and a coyote shapeshifter living in a world of werewolves, vampires, and fae, Mercy's independence, bravery, and moral compass make her an endearing protagonist. Her ability to navigate between different supernatural factions, coupled with her loyalty to her friends and her quest for justice, resonates with readers looking for characters with depth and integrity.

In *"The Mortal Instruments"* series by Cassandra Clare, Luke Garroway serves as a quintessential example of blending human sensibility with the formidable traits of a werewolf. Luke's unwavering loyalty to Clary and her mother and his leadership within the werewolf pack highlights his dual nature. His character demonstrates how compassion and strength coexist, providing Clary with a father figure amidst the chaos of the Shadow World. Luke's ability to navigate the complexities of both human and supernatural worlds makes him a relatable and admired character.

In the *"Women of the Otherworld"* series by Kelley Armstrong, Elena Michaels epitomizes the internal conflict and eventual acceptance of one's dual nature. As the only female werewolf, Elena's journey from rejection to embracing her identity offers readers a narrative of empowerment and self-discovery. Armstrong skillfully portrays Elena's vulnerabilities and strengths, her human desires against her werewolf instincts, creating a protagonist who resonates deeply with readers navigating their own identity struggles.

Alicia Montgomery's *"True Alpha"* series introduces us to characters who, despite their supernatural powers, deal with issues of trust, love, and societal expectations. The protagonists in these stories must navigate the challenges of leadership, loyalty, and love while balancing their human emotions with their responsibilities as alphas. Montgomery's characters are relatable because they reflect the universal struggle of adhering to one's values and desires in the face of external pressures and personal doubts.

The *"Alpha Girl"* series by Aileen Erin offers a fresh perspective on the coming-of-age narrative through its protagonist, Tessa McCaide. Transitioning into a new life as a werewolf while tackling the trials of high school, Tessa's character growth is a compelling exploration of identity, belonging, and the strength found in accepting oneself. Erin crafts Tessa's journey with sensitivity and depth, highlighting the importance of resilience and the power of found family.

In *"Moonbreeze"* from the "Dragonian Series" by Adrienne Woods, the protagonist's journey underscores the significance of embracing one's dual nature for personal empowerment and the greater good. The interplay between dragon and human aspects provides a rich canvas for exploring themes of identity, power, and love. Woods' narrative illustrates how the protagonist's struggles and triumphs resonate with readers, making her journey mirror our quests for self-acceptance and purpose.

The character of Ren from *"The Matefinder Series"* by Leia Stone exemplifies the balance of power and vulnerability. Ren's protective instincts and deep respect and love for his mate showcase the complexities of werewolf relationships. Stone adeptly navigates the intricacies of pack politics, loyalty, and the pursuit of happiness, creating a character who embodies strength, compassion, and unwavering dedication.

Creating solid and likable characters involves more than just detailing their supernatural abilities or human flaws; it requires a deep dive into their psyche, exploring how their dual nature affects their worldview, relationships, and choices. By drawing on the examples provided and focusing on the richness of your characters' experiences, you can craft protagonists who captivate the imagination and echo the complexities and resilience of the human spirit. Through this careful balance of human and werewolf traits, your characters will become the beating heart of your story, forging a connection with readers that endures long after the final page is turned.

Chapter 10

The Mate Bond

In the pulsing heart of a werewolf romance lies the chemistry of love, a potent mix of primal instinct and the deep, soulful connection that defines the mate bond. This bond is not merely a trope but a foundational element that elevates the romance plot, making it both intense and uniquely compelling. As we explore this chemistry, we uncover the layers that make werewolf romances stand apart, where the raw energy of the supernatural meets the timeless dance of attraction and love.

The mate bond is often depicted as an irresistible force, a connection so deep it transcends mere physical attraction. This bond is instinctual, a call of the wild that werewolves cannot ignore. It roots the romance in something ancient and powerful, giving it a predestined quality that speaks to the fantasy of finding one's perfect other half. The concept of 'fated mates' adds a layer of destiny to the relationship, making the journey of the characters not just about love but about fulfilling a destiny written in the stars—or, in this case, the moon's light.

However, the chemistry of romance in these stories is not just about the inevitability of the mate bond. It's also about the tension and the conflict it introduces. The idea that one has no choice but to feel drawn to another can create internal struggles, especially for characters who value their independence or have been hurt in the past. This conflict adds depth to the romance, making the eventual acceptance of the bond a journey of personal growth and healing.

Moreover, the mate bond often involves heightened emotions and senses, intensifying every glance, touch, and word spoken. This sensory amplification makes the romantic connection between the characters incredibly vivid for readers. The ability to sense each other's emotions or even thoughts adds an intimate layer to their beautiful and challenging relationship, as there's nowhere to hide in such closeness.

The physical aspect of the mate bond in werewolf romances is undeniably compelling. The primal attraction, the sense of belonging only to each other, is a powerful draw for readers. It's not just about passion but also the comfort and safety found in one's mate—the feeling of coming home. This physicality is balanced with tender moments of vulnerability and care, creating a well-rounded depiction of a relationship. Let's look at some examples of how the mate bond works:

In Nalini Singh's *Psy-Changeling* series, the concept of the mate bond takes on a profound significance. The series presents a world where changelings (shapeshifters) experience a deep, almost telepathic connection with their mates. This bond is not just about attraction but also about a profound emotional and psychic link. Singh explores how the mate bond can be both a strength and a vulnerability, offering characters like Lucas and Sascha or Hawke and Sienna a depth of understanding and unity that's unparalleled, yet also exposing them to new forms of danger and challenges, particularly from those who seek to exploit or destroy the bond.

In Patricia Briggs' *Mercy Thompson* series, the mate bond is depicted as focusing on choice and mutual respect, alongside the instinctual pull werewolves feel towards their mates. Briggs crafts a world where the bond doesn't override personal agency, providing an interesting commentary on the balance between fate and free will. Characters like Adam and Mercy navigate their relationship with an awareness of the bond's influence. Yet, their story emphasizes the importance of consent and mutual decision-making, portraying a bond that strengthens their partnership rather than diminishes their individuality.

The Black Dagger Brotherhood series by J.R. Ward show-cases the mate bond as a transformative force. In this series, the bond is often a catalyst for personal growth and healing. Characters like Zsadist, who is deeply scarred by his past, find in the mate bond not just love but a path to healing and redemption. Ward delves into the complexities of accepting the bond, especially for individuals broken by life, making the mate bond a journey of overcoming inner demons and learning to trust and love again.

Kelley Armstrong's *Otherworld* series explores the mate bond through characters like Elena and Clay. Armstrong portrays the bond as deeply instinctual yet fraught with human complications. Their relationship, rooted in a turbulent history and the challenges of navigating life as were-wolves, showcases the tension between the natural pull of the bond and the realities of their past actions and decisions. This series emphasizes that the mate bond, while powerful, is not a simple solution to personal issues but rather a component of a larger, more complex relationship that requires work, understanding, and forgiveness.

"The Wolves of Mercy Falls" series by Maggie Stiefvater presents a poignant exploration of the mate bond with a twist, focusing on the love story between Sam and Grace. Unlike the typical werewolf lore, their connection, while not termed as a customary 'mate bond' in werewolf terms, echoes the concept's depth and inevitability. Their relation-ship is marked by a sense of recognition and a pull towards

each other that defies normal human relationships, capturing the essence of the mate bond in a subtle yet powerful manner. Stiefvater's portrayal emphasizes such a bond's emotional and psychological aspects, showcasing how it can challenge and complete the individuals involved.

"Moon Called" by Patricia Briggs, part of the Mercy Thompson series, introduces readers to a world where the mate bond is both a source of strength and a complex challenge. While the series primarily revolves around Mercy's relationships and heritage, it also delves into the dynamics of the werewolf packs and their leaders. The bond between Alpha werewolf Adam Hauptman and Mercy evolves, showcasing how the mate bond can be acknowledged and accepted in stages rather than instantaneously, adding layers to their relationship and highlighting the importance of choice and consent within the supernatural framework.

In *the "Alpha & Omega"* series, also by Patricia Briggs, the concept of the mate bond is further explored through Charles and Anna. Their bond is immediate and profound, providing Anna with a sense of safety and understanding she's never known. Briggs beautifully illustrates how the mate bond can serve as a healing force, particularly for Anna, who comes from a background of abuse. The series emphasizes the protective and empathetic aspects of the bond, showcasing its power to heal and empower individuals to become their best selves.

"Feral Sins" by Suzanne Wright, the first book in *The Phoenix Pack Series,* dives into the passionate and tumultuous relationship between Taryn and Trey. Their mate bond is intense, filled with fiery clashes and deep, undeniable connections. Wright explores the dynamics of power, control, and vulnerability within the mate bond, portraying it as a multifaceted relationship that requires negotiation, understanding, and growth. The series stands out for its portrayal of the mate bond as not just a magical connection but as a partnership that evolves and strengthens through adversity.

While broader than werewolf lore, Sherrilyn Kenyon's *"Dark Hunter" series incorporates predestined bond* elements through its diverse characters, including shapeshifters. The concept of fated mates runs parallel to the mate bond, creating intense and soul-deep connections that transcend time and challenges. Kenyon's approach to the mate bond-like connections is rich with themes of redemption, sacrifice, and the transformative power of love, adding a dark and mystical glamour to the narrative.

"The Mating" by Nicky Charles takes readers into the heart of werewolf society, where the mate bond is not only a personal connection but also a matter of pack politics and social stability. The relationship between Elise and Bryan challenges the age-old notions of the mate bond, introducing elements of choice, duty, and societal expectations into the mix. Charles' exploration of the mate bond within the

context of pack dynamics and individual desires adds a compelling layer of complexity to the romance, highlighting the tension between personal happiness and communal responsibility.

"Shifters Unbound" series by Jennifer Ashley - In this series, Ashley introduces a world where shifters are known to the public and live under strict laws. The mate bond here is portrayed with a mix of destiny and choice, highlighting the struggles shifters face in a society that fears them. Characters like Liam Morrissey and Kim Fraser in "Pride Mates" navigate the complexities of shifter-human relationships, with the mate bond challenging societal prejudices and personal barriers, reinforcing the idea that love can transcend boundaries.

"The Nightshade Series" by Andrea Cremer - Cremer's narrative delves into the world of Guardians, who can shift into wolves, and the Witches who guide them. The series explores not just the romantic aspect of the mate bond but also its political and social implications within the secretive world of the Keepers. Calla and Ren's story, set against a backdrop of duty and rebellion, examines how the mate bond can be both a gift and a curse, a source of strength and a point of vulnerability.

"New Moon" from the *"Twilight Saga"* by Stephenie Meyer - While primarily focused on vampires, this saga also explores the concept of werewolves and their unique bonding, specifically through the character of Jacob Black. Meyer introduces a form of the mate bond through the Quileute shapeshifters, which, while different from classic werewolf lore, emphasizes the themes of unrequited love and the pain of being close to someone destined for another. Jacob's complex feelings for Bella offer a poignant look at the mate bond's emotional dimensions, exploring the heartache and loyalty that come with it.

"The Bourbon Kings" by J.R. Ward - Though not a werewolf series, J.R. Ward's portrayal of intense, almost fated love relationships echoes the depth and complexity of the mate bond in her paranormal works. The series, set in the opulent world of Kentucky bourbon moguls, explores themes of loyalty, family legacy, and the enduring power of love, reminiscent of the emotional landscapes navigated in werewolf mate bonds. Ward's skill in incorporating tales of love against the odds shines through, offering a human parallel to the supernatural bond found in her "Black Dagger Brotherhood" series.

"Dragon Bound" by Thea Harrison - Part of the "Elder Races" series, this book, while focusing on dragons and other creatures, touches upon the idea of fated mates with its dragon-shifter hero. Harrison crafts a world where magical beings find their one true mate, a concept that, while not exclusive to werewolves, shares the mate bond's essence in werewolf romance. The relationship between Pia and Dragos explores trust, power dynamics, and the inevitable

pull of destined love, showcasing how the mate bond transcends species boundaries in paranormal romance.

As seen, the chemistry of the werewolf romance genre encompasses the struggle for autonomy within the mate bond. Characters often grapple with the fear of losing their identity or being consumed by the bond. This struggle for balance between the self and the union adds a relatable human element to the supernatural romance, making it richer and more complex.

In addition to the mate bond, chemistry is refined by the pack dynamics. The interaction with the pack, with its own set of rules and relationships, provides a backdrop that can either support or challenge the primary romance. The need to protect, belong, or defy the pack adds layers of external conflict and solidarity that test and strengthen the bond between the mates.

The role of the alpha also plays a significant part in the chemistry. The alpha's strength, leadership, and responsibility to the pack often clash with the romantic relationship's vulnerabilities and needs, creating tension that must be navigated. The balance between power and tenderness, dominance, and equality builds the romance, making it a dance of give and take.

The concept of the lunar cycle and its influence introduces a rhythmic ebb and flow to the romance and its chemistry. The full moon, with its call to the wolf, can act as a catalyst for revealing emotions, deepening the connection, or bringing to the surface hidden conflicts. This cyclical nature mirrors the ups and downs of a love affair, adding a naturalistic dimension to the romantic plot.

Introducing rivalries or external threats can also heighten the chemistry between the protagonists. The need to protect each other or to face challenges together solidifies their bond, making every triumph and every shared vulnerability a step closer to a deeper connection. This external pressure tests the mate bond, proving that it is not just destiny but a choice to fight for each other.

Werewolf romances often explore the notion of healing and redemption through love. The mate bond becomes a path to healing old wounds, overcoming past traumas, and finding acceptance. This journey of healing together, of finding strength in each other, adds an emotional depth that resonates with readers personally.

Moreover, the characters' interplay of human and werewolf personas balances their love affair. The blend of human vulnerability with the werewolf's strength and loyalty creates relatable yet admirably resilient characters. Their story is a testament to the power of love to bridge worlds, heal, and transform.

The enduring fascination behind these stories lies in the promise of unconditional love and acceptance within the mate bond. It's a love that sees beyond the surface, recognizing the soul beneath. This unconditional acceptance is the ultimate fantasy, making werewolf romances a beloved escape for readers seeking stories where love is not just a feeling but a destiny fulfilled.

Chapter 11

Obstacles & Tensions

In the world of werewolves, the path to true love is never straightforward. Obstacles and tensions are not merely hurdles to be cleared; they're the very elements that add spice and depth to the story, making the eventual union all the more satisfying. As you write the tale of two souls destined to be together, remember that the challenges they face are what transform a simple narrative into a compelling saga of love, growth, and triumph.

Firstly, consider the clash of worlds. Imagine your protagonist, perhaps a human unknowingly stepping into the hidden world of werewolves or a werewolf struggling to maintain their secret existence. This collision of realities is fertile ground for conflict, as each character must navigate the complexities of a life they were unprepared for. The journey of understanding and acceptance between such different beings provides a rich narrative vein to mine, filled with potential misunderstandings, prejudices to overcome, and the thrill of discovering the unknown.

Then there's the internal struggle, a potent source of romantic tension. A werewolf might grapple with the fear of endangering their beloved due to their more primal instincts. At the same time, their human counterpart might battle insecurities about fitting into a world vastly different from their own. This internal conflict adds layers to your characters' journey toward each other, making their journey as much about personal growth as it is about love. It's a reminder that the road to love often starts with learning to navigate one's fears and doubts.

Family and pack dynamics offer another rich seam of conflict. The expectations and traditions of a werewolf pack can impose heavy burdens on your characters, especially if their love crosses forbidden lines. Perhaps there's a rivalry between packs or a family curse that dooms love to fail. These external pressures test the strength of your characters' bond, challenging them to stand united against the world or risk losing each other forever.

The presence of a rival can also intensify the romantic tension. This could be a suitor from within the pack who challenges the bond between your protagonists or an outside threat that forces them to confront their feelings for each other. The jealousy and fear of loss can act as catalysts, pushing your characters to realize the depth of their connection and fight for their love with renewed determination.

The supernatural element itself is a treasure trove of conflict. The unique abilities and weaknesses of being a werewolf can lead to complex ethical dilemmas and physical challenges. Perhaps there's a curse to break or a prophecy that predicts dire consequences for their union. These supernatural obstacles add excitement and mystery to your narrative and provide opportunities for your characters to demonstrate their courage, resourcefulness, and unwavering commitment to each other.

Then, there's the battle for acceptance within and outside the werewolf community. The struggle to have their love recognized and respected by others can be a significant source of tension. It's a fight for the right to love freely, challenging societal norms and prejudices, and in doing so, your characters can become symbols of hope and change for themselves and the world they inhabit.

Consider these book scenarios:

In the book, *"Wolf Rain"* by Nalini Singh, part of the Psy-Changeling Trinity series, the characters Alexei and Memory face external threats and the daunting task of overcoming personal traumas. Memory, with her unique E-Psy abilities, finds herself targeted by nefarious forces. At the same time, Alexei grapples with the fear that he might succumb to the same madness that afflicted his family. Their journey is a poignant exploration of trust and healing, showcasing how love can emerge stronger through the crucible of shared struggles and mutual support.

"The Last Wolf" by Maria Vale is set in a world where the Silver Nirs live hidden from human eyes, bound by strict laws and traditions. The protagonist, Silver, is considered weak and half-wild. Still, her encounter with Tiberius, a lone shifter with a mysterious past, sets them on a collision course with pack laws and external dangers. Their relationship challenges the very foundations of their society, highlighting how love can inspire one to question long-held beliefs and fight for a future that once seemed impossible.

The story *"Cry Wolf"* by Patricia Briggs, opening the Alpha and Omega series, introduces Anna and Charles, who must navigate not only their new, unexpected bond but also a threat that could destroy the pack. Anna, a rare Omega wolf with the power to calm others, is still recovering from years of abuse. At the same time, Charles, the enforcer, must reconcile his protective instincts with respect for Anna's strength. Their mission to confront a rogue werewolf becomes a journey of mutual healing, illustrating how external conflicts can mirror and magnify the internal growth of characters.

In *"How to Flirt with a Naked Werewolf"* by Molly Harper, the story combines humor with tension as Mo Wenstein moves to Grundy, Alaska, seeking peace but finds herself entangled with Cooper Graham, a werewolf struggling with his own demons. Their romance, filled with witty banter and humorous situations, also touches on serious themes such as independence, acceptance, and the courage to face one's fears. Blending light-hearted moments with deeper conflicts creates a dynamic and engaging narrative.

"Prince of Wolves" by Quinn Loftis introduces readers to a world where the bond between mates is both a blessing and a challenge. Jacque and Fane's instant connection is fraught with difficulties, from cultural differences to the threat posed by an alpha from another pack who claims Jacque as his own. Their story is a testament to the strength found in unity and the power of love to overcome prejudice and rivalry.

"Moonlight" by Lisa Kessler, part of the Moon series, explores the tension between duty and desire. Lana, a werewolf hunter, and Adam, the pack's alpha, are drawn together by a bond they neither expected nor understood. Their relationship is a forbidden dance of attraction and resistance against a centuries-old feud. The story skillfully uses the theme of forbidden love to heighten the stakes, forcing the characters to confront their loyalties and desires.

"Wolf Signs" by Vivian Arend focuses on Robyn and Keil. Robyn, unknowingly a werewolf, and Keil, tasked with teaching her about her heritage, find themselves in a secluded cabin during a snowstorm. The isolation serves as

a backdrop for physical and emotional discovery, highlighting the importance of communication and consent within the mate bond. Their story is a compelling exploration of identity and the journey to self-acceptance, made worthier by their challenges.

Remember, the essence of a great werewolf romance story lies not in avoiding obstacles but in facing and overcoming them. Each challenge, each moment of tension, is a step on the journey that shapes your characters and their relationship. Through these trials, their love is tested, strengthened, and ultimately proven unbreakable.

Chapter 12

Hitting your Tropes

Tropes always serve as the backbone of many beloved storylines. Yet the true artistry lies in how these conventions are used and twisted, breathing new life into age-old narratives. To keep your stories vibrant and engaging, consider embracing and subverting these common themes, thus offering readers a fresh take on the genre they adore.

The most common trope is the 'fated mates' concept, where werewolves find their perfect other half through an instant and unbreakable supernatural bond. You might introduce characters who initially resist or doubt the bond to subvert this. This resistance can stem from personal traumas, a desire for independence, or skepticism towards destiny. By allowing your characters to question and even fight against the bond, you create a more dynamic relationship development. For example, imagine a scenario where the protagonists, after being irresistibly drawn together, decide to separate to pursue personal goals or to ensure that their bond is not merely destiny but a choice. This journey back to each other, armed with a deeper understanding of themselves and what they truly desire, can offer a nuanced exploration of love and fate.

Another one is the alpha werewolf—dominant, protective, and often possessing a controlling nature. While this character type can be compelling, flipping this trope on its head can offer readers something unexpected. Consider crafting a story around a beta or an omega who rises to leadership or becomes the protagonist's love interest. This character could use intelligence, empathy, and cunning rather than brute strength to protect and lead. Such a story challenges the archetypal power dynamics and celebrates different forms of strength and leadership, providing a refreshing take on the werewolf pack hierarchy.

The 'lone wolf' trope, in which a werewolf is ostracized from or chooses to leave their pack, is also ripe for subversion. Instead of following the conventional narrative of loneliness and longing for a return, you could depict a lone wolf who thrives in solitude or finds a new sense of family among non-werewolves or other supernatural beings. This character's journey can redefine the concept of pack and belonging, emphasizing the idea that family and community are not just about blood or species but about mutual respect and love.

Werewolf romances often feature conflict stemming from external threats—rival packs, hunters, or supernatural enemies. While these elements heighten tension, consider subverting this trope by focusing on internal pack dynamics or personal growth as the main source of conflict. Perhaps the story revolves around political intrigue within the pack or the protagonist's struggle with their identity as a werewolf. This shift from external to internal conflict can deepen character development and offer a more introspective take on the werewolf experience.

The transformation, often portrayed as a painful, uncontrollable curse, offers another opportunity for subversion. Imagine a world where transformation is celebrated as a rite of passage or a cherished gift, with rituals and ceremonies that highlight the beauty and power of shifting. This positive portrayal can change the narrative from fear and loathing to empowerment and pride, exploring themes of acceptance and the celebration of one's true nature.

The notion of werewolves being violent or savage can be flipped by presenting werewolf society as one that values peace, diplomacy, and human coexistence. In this narrative, werewolves might be protectors of the natural world or mediators between the supernatural and human realms. This approach challenges stereotypes and opens avenues for exploring themes of environmentalism, peacekeeping, and the nuanced balance between human and animal instincts.

Chapter 13

Tensions

Mastering writing tension through your narratives is paramount for gripping your readers' attention and keeping them in suspense. As a connoisseur of narratives pulsating with the heartbeats of humans and mythical creatures, diving into the intricacies of tension amplifiers is essential. These narrative mechanisms do more than embellish your story; they are its backbone, infusing your tale with vitality and enabling it to spring forth with unforeseen intensity.

Secrets wield immense power as catalysts for tension. The deeper and more dangerous the secret, the more it imbues your story with a promise of dramatic revelations. Picture a protagonist burdened with a clandestine truth about their lineage, oblivious to their rightful place at the helm of a formidable pack or holding information that could either mend fractious factions or deepen their divides. Such secrets foster a compelling sense of suspense, propelling readers through the pages in anticipation of the revelatory moment and its consequences. The *"Alpha Girl"* series by Aileen Erin exemplifies the artful use of secrets, with concealed histories and taboo knowledge carving out the destinies of its characters.

The trope of forbidden love invariably injects intensity into the narrative. The enticement of a love that breaches societal, familial, or pack-imposed barriers echoes with the thrill of defiance and the peril of exposure. A romance fraught with danger, where each clandestine encounter is a gambit against formidable adversaries, accelerates the pulse. This trope is fervently navigated in Rebecca Zanetti's *"Dark Protectors"* series, showcasing how love can challenge and transcend imposed boundaries.

Moreover, internal and external rivalries introduce a compelling layer of tension. A rival presents a tangible obstacle to the protagonist's objectives, embodying and personalizing the conflict. Conflicts over leadership, affection, or mere survival, especially when the rival is a formidable match, perfect the narrative. Such rivalries, even those tinged with respect and understanding, are illustrated through the complex interplay of factions in Patricia Briggs' *"Mercy Thompson"* series.

The element of time, or its scarcity, emerges as a crucial amplifier of tension. A looming deadline, such as the arrival of a full moon heralding uncontrollable transformation, a curse that must be lifted by daybreak, or an impending prophecy's fulfillment, propels characters into decisive action. It forces them to confront the repercussions of their choices, often made under duress. Kelley Armstrong's *"Otherworld"* series adeptly uses time as a crucible for character development and narrative progression.

Integrating moral quandaries further heightens the stakes, introducing psychological tension. Characters grapple with decisions fraught with significant repercussions, engaging readers in their moral dilemmas. Whether it involves accepting one's werewolf nature at the potential cost of human connections or protecting loved ones at a greater societal cost, these dilemmas test characters' morals and desires, as depicted in the *"Shifter's Shadow"* series by Elle Thorne.

The inherent unpredictability of the werewolf nature itself naturally escalates tension. Highlighting the battle for control during transformations or intense emotional episodes adds a layer of unpredictability and danger. Anne Bishop's *"Others"* series effectively captures this wild unpredictability, reminding readers of the primal forces simmering beneath the surface, boosting the narrative with suspense and unpredictability.

External adversaries infuse the storyline with immediate tension, from hunters to rival supernatural entities. These antagonists pose threats to the pack's safety, challenge alliances, and endanger the protagonists' peace. Facing a common foe can unify characters in surprising ways, strengthening bonds through adversity. Nalini Singh's *"Psy-Changeling"* series illustrates how external dangers can foster relationships and drive the story, creating a rich narrative of alliances, betrayals, and survival.

Finally, exploring themes of identity and acceptance within the pack and the wider society adds emotional depth and tension. The quest for self-acceptance, the anxiety of exclusion, and the struggle for belonging deeply resonate with readers, mirroring universal experiences through the supernatural prism. Though focused on vampires, Lynsay Sands' *"Argeneau"* series tackles themes of identity, belonging, and the supernatural-human divide, offering valuable insights for werewolf romance narratives.

By adeptly incorporating these tension amplifiers into your story, your werewolf romance transcends mere events to become an enthralling epic that captivates readers from start to finish. The secret lies in layering these elements, allowing them to enhance one another and crafting a rich, complex, and irresistibly engaging narrative.

Chapter 14

Writing Action Scenes

Writing about werewolf transformations and their showdowns requires a knack for detail and a deep dive into the emotional and physical stakes at play. It's more than just the thrill of the moment; it's about moving the story forward and peeling back layers of character development. Let's get into how you can bring these scenes to life with authenticity and heart-pounding excitement, keeping your readers on the edge of their seats.

The atmosphere is crucial in setting the scene for a transformation or a face-off. The setting plays a huge role in cranking up the tension and drama. Picture the scene in an eerie, dense forest under a full moon or on a lonely mountain ridge—these backdrops can dial up the suspense and highlight the werewolf's raw nature. Dive into the sensory details—the moonlight dances through the trees, the earthy scent of pine, and the eerie howls in the distance. These touches can pull readers into the action, making it feel palpable.

Capturing a werewolf transformation is all about the gritty details of the process. It's a visceral, often agonizing experience that pushes the boundaries of the character's body and mind. Describing how limbs stretch, bones reshape, and senses heighten can bring out the sheer power and pain of the change. But don't forget the emotional rollercoaster— the fear, the rush, or the sense of release that comes with the transformation. Tackling both the physical and emotional aspects makes the scene hit harder, showing the inner battle that comes with embracing the beast within.

When it comes to showdowns, think dynamic and strategic. These aren't just brawls but intelligent, intuitive, tactical fights. Clear, sharp descriptions focusing on key movements and strategies keep the action engaging without getting lost. Showcase the werewolves' supernatural abilities—speed, agility, and raw power—to make each confrontation a spectacle.

Being true to the world you've built is crucial. Set the ground rules early—how werewolves heal, their strengths, their Achilles' heel. If silver is their weakness, the mere sight of a silver weapon can ramp up the suspense. If the bond between mates boosts their strength, let that connection swing the momentum of a fight. These details better the story and keep the supernatural elements consistent and believable.

Don't overlook the psychological and emotional stakes. Fear, anger, desperation, and even a sense of honor can deeply influence characters' decisions during these high-stakes moments. Addressing the consequences of their actions, whether dealing with loss, facing the repercussions of leading a pack into danger, or coping with emotional trauma, adds layers to the narrative.

Post-battle, it's crucial to explore the fallout—physical exhaustion, changes in pack dynamics, or emotional wounds. These scenes illuminate the characters' resilience, empathy, and inner conflict, intensifying the story.

Incorporating different viewpoints can also add depth and excitement. Experiencing a transformation or battle through various characters' eyes can give a fuller understanding and build suspense as readers put the pieces together.

Balance is essential. Remember, these action-packed moments should propel the story, offer character insights, and flesh out the world you've created. Each scene should have a purpose, whether to showcase a character's strengths or vulnerabilities, test relationships or steer the story to its peak.

By thoughtfully interweaving these elements, you can create action scenes that thrill with intensity and resonate on an emotional level. These moments become key to your characters' journeys, reflecting their inner struggles, primal nature, and profoundly human hearts.

Chapter 15

Intimacy, Conflict & Resolution

Writing moments of intimacy, conflict, and resolution in a werewolf romance requires a delicate touch, balancing the raw, primal aspects of werewolf lore with the deep emotional currents that drive the human heart. These moments, whether tender, tumultuous, or transformative, are the keystones of your narrative, offering readers a glimpse into the very soul of your characters. Let's navigate this complex terrain, ensuring your story resonates with authenticity and emotional depth.

Intimacy in werewolf romance transcends the physical, weaving in the supernatural elements that define your characters. The first brush of intimacy often comes layered with the heightened senses of a werewolf— a touch isn't just felt on the skin but reverberates through the soul. Describing these initial moments with attention to the werewolf's acute senses— the smell of rain on their partner's skin, the sound of a quickened heartbeat, the electric touch of skin on fur— can elevate the scene, making it visceral. Drawing on the unique aspects of werewolf physiology can deepen the connection, making the moment about closeness and recognition and acceptance of each other's true natures.

When depicting conflict, remember that the stakes in werewolf romance are often higher due to the dual nature of your characters. Conflicts can stem from external pressures— rival packs, human threats, supernatural politics—but the most compelling conflicts often arise from internal struggles. A werewolf grappling with their nature, fearing the beast within will harm those they love, offers a profound layer of emotional complexity. Portray these conflicts honestly, diving into the character's psyche and letting their fears, doubts, and desires drive the narrative. The conflict between their werewolf instincts and human emotions can be a powerful metaphor for the universal struggle between duty and desire, fear and love.

Resolving these conflicts requires a journey that challenges both the werewolf and their human side. Resolution doesn't always mean a happy ending in the traditional sense but should always involve growth and change. Perhaps your character learns to accept their dual nature, finding balance and peace within themselves, which allows them to open up to love and intimacy. Alternatively, resolution might come through sacrifice, a decision that underscores the depth of their feelings. This sacrifice, whether it's giving up power, leaving a pack, or exposing themselves to danger, should be a testament to their love's strength and the courage of their convictions.

Moments of intimacy after conflict should reflect the journey your characters have undergone. These scenes are not just physical reunions but emotional reconciliations, where the characters come together stronger and more deeply connected for the trials they've faced. Describing these scenes should involve all the senses, emphasizing the emotional and physical relief of being reunited. The texture of a caress, the warmth of a kiss, or the grounding sensation of the other's scent can all convey the depth of their connection.

In a werewolf romance, transformations can be moments of vulnerability and trust, especially when shared with a partner. Writing these scenes with emotional depth means capturing the awe, fear, and acceptance that comes with witnessing such a profound change. The transformation is both a letting go and a coming into power, and describing it should involve both the physical sensations—the pain, the rush of strength, the sudden sharpness of senses—and the emotional turmoil and eventual acceptance accompanying it.

Confrontations in these stories are not just physical battles but emotional turning points. Whether it's a showdown with an antagonist or a challenge within the pack, these confrontations are charged with the history and emotions of your characters. Writing these scenes requires a careful balance of action and emotion, where every blow struck, and every wound received is as much about the characters' internal battles as their external ones. The outcome of these confrontations should feel earned, the result of both physical prowess and emotional growth.

Make sure you write with emotional depth, which means not shying away from the messiness of emotions. Characters in a werewolf romance, with their heightened senses and instincts, experience feelings with an intensity that can be overwhelming. Their anger burns hotter, their love more consuming, their grief more profound. Capturing this intensity without losing the nuance of their human side is key. The true depth of their feelings is revealed in the moments of quiet, the gentle touches, the whispered confessions, and the shared looks.

Take note of the resolution in a werewolf romance, which often involves a new understanding or balance between your characters' werewolf and human aspects. This doesn't mean the erasure of conflict but accepting it as part of who they are. Writing this resolution requires reflecting on the journey, highlighting how the struggles have shaped the characters and their relationship. It's a celebration of survival and love, acknowledging that while the future may hold more challenges, the characters are better equipped to face them together.

Whether a grand gesture or a simple moment of understanding, the story's final act should come back to your narrative's core themes. This scene is a culmination of their emotional journey, a testament to their bond, strengthened not despite but because of the challenges they've overcome. Crafting this moment with an emphasis on emotional truth can leave a lasting impression on your readers.

Your story can resonate deeply with readers by carefully adding intimacy, conflict, and resolution, woven with the unique threads of werewolf lore and human emotion. In these moments, charged with authenticity and depth, the heart of werewolf romance beats strongest, offering tales of love that are as wild and beautiful as the moonlit creatures at their center.

Chapter 16

Balance Action & Romance

In the heart-pounding world of werewolf romance, striking the right balance between edge-of-your-seat action and swoon-worthy romance is crucial for keeping your readers hooked. This delicate balance ensures your story isn't just a page-turner but also deeply resonates with your characters' emotional journeys, marrying moments of adrenaline with those of heartfelt connection. Let's dive into how to craft a narrative that beats with life, masterfully choreographing the dance between the call of the wild and the whispers of the heart.

Kick things off by setting the stakes high from the get-go. Your opening scenes should tease the brewing romance and hint at the action ahead, gripping your readers' emotions and piquing their curiosity. Picture this: a seemingly ordinary moment between two characters on the cusp of love, suddenly disrupted by a surprise attack. This blend of action and emotional connection hooks your readers from the start, promising them a ride through danger and desire.

Developing well-rounded characters is key to navigating the action-romance balance. Your characters must be warriors in one breath and lovers in the next, their battles reflecting their innermost struggles and desires. Let their combative moments serve as extensions of their personal stories. When they fight to protect someone dear or save themselves, it deepens the action, making every conflict reflect their emotional battles.

Pacing is your narrative's heartbeat. Think of your story like a symphony, with high-octane action sequences and tender romantic moments following each other in a rhythm that boosts the tale. After an intense action scene, give your characters (and readers) a breather, a chance for romantic elements to bubble up and take shape. This push and pull keeps readers engaged, balancing the thrill of battle with the depth of emotional connection.

Let action scenes be more than just adrenaline; use them as opportunities for character growth and relationship development. A brush with danger can strip away barriers, prompting confessions of love or confronting the fear of loss. These moments tie the excitement of survival directly to the vulnerability of love, layering your story with a rich emotional tapestry.

In the same vein, ensure that the intimacy between characters shapes how they face their battles. The strength they draw from quiet moments of connection should be their beacon in the chaos of conflict. This mutual influence binds the action and romance together, propelling each other forward.

Dialogue is your secret weapon for bridging action and romance. It can seamlessly transition your story from a heart-pounding fight to a moment of softness. Let your characters voice their fears, dreams, and love amid their turbulent world, keeping the emotional narrative in step with the physical action.

The setting also plays a crucial role in harmonizing action and romance. Choose environments that reflect or contrast your characters' internal states—a tranquil hideaway for intimate moments, a stormy battlefield mirroring their turmoil. The environment isn't just a backdrop but an active force that heightens the emotional stakes of each scene.

Conflict resolution keeps your story moving. Every action-packed challenge should lead to emotional growth or revelations, fueling the romantic arc. Conversely, resolving romantic tensions should naturally open new avenues for action, driving the plot toward its climax. This interplay ensures your narrative remains dynamic, with each element propelling the story forward.

At its core, a compelling werewolf romance is about characters growing stronger through adversity, both in love and battle. Their triumphs and trials forge a bond that's as unyielding as their resolve, making each victory meaningful and their love enduring.

You'll craft a tale that captivates and moves your readers by skillfully intertwining action and romance, mindful of pacing, character arcs, and emotional depth. The entwining of danger and desire will have your readers hanging on every word, eagerly flipping pages to discover how the dance between love and action plays out to the very end.

Chapter 17

Final Thoughts

As we close, I want to share a few thoughts that I hope will stick with you as you start writing romances that will capture and enchant your readers. Writing, just like the werewolves we love, is constantly changing, pushing you to be both brave and open.

The world of werewolves is as broad as your imagination. It's a place where wild hearts and gentle feelings collide, where not only do physical battles rage across landscapes, but emotional battles rage within the hearts of our beloved characters. Your voice can bring fresh life to this genre, telling stories that dive deep into the emotions, desires, and relentless search for love that defines both humans and werewolves.

Face the challenges head-on; they are just milestones on your way to greatness. Each challenge you overcome, every doubt you push past, strengthens your voice and enriches your stories. Like the characters you create, you will grow with every story you tell and every word you write.

Don't be afraid to mix things up, to explore the unknown corners of your imagination. The stories that stick with us are those that take what we know and turn it into something new and exciting. Your unique view is precious, sparking innovation and passion in werewolf romance.

When you find yourself struggling for inspiration, remember why you started on this path. Remember the first romance that captured your heart, making it race and ache with longing. You can spark those same feelings in your readers, creating worlds and characters that stay with them long after they've finished reading.

Most of all, write with love—love for the act of writing, for your characters, and for the stories that only you can tell. Let this love guide you through the tough times of writer's block and through any criticism you might face. For it's love that's at the core of all great werewolf romances—the kind of love that defies all odds, turning the ordinary into something magical and bringing us together through stories.

As you stand ready to start your next book, remember you're not alone. A community of readers and writers who share your love for romance is behind you, excited to see where your creativity will lead. So, take a deep breath. The world is eager for your stories, for your voice to join the ongoing writing genre of paranormal romance.

Write fearlessly, write boldly, and let your imagination take flight. In the world of werewolf romance, the sky's the limit. Here's to the stories you'll create, the hearts you'll move, and the journey ahead. May it be as magical and transformative as the tales you're about to write.

Glossary

Alpha: The leader of a werewolf pack. Alphas are responsible for the safety and well-being of their pack members and are often characterized by strong leadership qualities and formidable strength.

Beta: A high-ranking member of the pack who serves directly under the alpha, often acting as the second in command. Betas are trusted members of the pack with leadership responsibilities.

Omega: The lowest-ranking member of a werewolf pack. Omegas often serve as peacemakers within the pack and can hold unique roles depending on the story's context.

Pack: A group of werewolves living, hunting, and operating together as a family unit. Packs are bound by strict hierarchies and social rules.

Lone Wolf: A werewolf that lives outside of pack structures, either by choice or because of being ostracized. Pack-affiliated werewolves often view lone wolves with suspicion.

Mate Bond: A profound and mystical connection between werewolves, believed to be fated or predestined. The mate bond is characterized by intense emotional and physical connections.

Shifting: The process by which a human transforms into their werewolf form. Depending on the story, this can be influenced by emotional states, lunar cycles, or voluntary control.

Moon Called: The heightened state of power or compulsion that werewolves experience during the full moon. This period can affect a werewolf's strength, aggression, and ability to shift.

Silver Weakness: A common trope in werewolf lore where werewolves are vulnerable or weakened by silver, often leading to it being used as a weapon against them.

Territory: The geographic area claimed by a werewolf pack. Territories are marked and defended against rivals or threats.

Rogue: A werewolf who does not belong to any pack and does not follow the typical werewolf codes of conduct.

Rogues can be antagonists or misunderstood characters in werewolf romances.

True Form: The werewolf's wolf-like appearance is distinct from its human form. The true form can vary in size, color, and features across different stories.

Human Form: The human appearance of a werewolf, in which they can blend into human society. Werewolves in human form retain some of their enhanced abilities, such as heightened senses.

Pack Bonds: The emotional and psychic connections between members of the same pack. These bonds can enhance communication, loyalty, and strength among pack members.

Blood Moon: A rare and significant event in werewolf lore, often associated with powerful shifts, heightened abilities, or significant pack rituals. The Blood Moon can also signify important turning points in werewolf prophecies or legends.

Challenge: A formal confrontation within werewolf society often used to settle disputes, determine hierarchy, or challenge the current alpha's leadership. Depending on the pack's customs, challenges can be physical or mental.

Curse: In some stories, becoming a werewolf is the result of a curse rather than a natural or hereditary condition. The specifics of the curse can vary, including its origins, effects, and the possibility of reversal.

Enforcer: A role within the pack dedicated to maintaining order, enforcing the alpha's laws, and protecting pack territory from intruders or threats. Enforcers are typically skilled fighters and loyal to their alpha.

Feral State: A condition in which a werewolf loses control over its human consciousness and becomes fully wolf in mind and body. This state can be triggered by extreme stress, anger, or the influence of the full moon.

Guardian: A werewolf or a group of werewolves tasked with protecting a specific person, place, or object of importance. Guardians are often chosen for their strength, loyalty, and dedication.

Lunar Influence: The effect that phases of the moon have on werewolf physiology and behavior. While the full moon is most commonly associated with transformations, other phases might influence moods, powers, or healing abilities.

Marking: A ritual or act where werewolves claim their mates or territory, often through a bite or a scratch. Marking can have both physical and mystical implications, signifying a deep bond or ownership.

Moonstone: A mystical gemstone that, in some stories, has the power to affect werewolves, either by enhancing their abilities, offering protection, or even curing the werewolf condition.

Nightshade: In some werewolf lore, a substance or plant that is toxic or harmful to werewolves, similar to the way silver is traditionally depicted. Nightshade's effects can range from weakening a werewolf to being lethal.

Pup: A term of endearment for a young werewolf or the child of werewolves. Pups are often raised with the protection of the entire pack, reflecting the communal nature of werewolf society.

Ritual: Ceremonies or practices with significant cultural or mystical importance in werewolf society. Rituals may be related to the moon cycles, rites of passage, healing, or mating practices.

Shaman: A werewolf or human with the ability to connect with supernatural forces. Shamans often serve as healers, spiritual guides, or advisors within werewolf communities. They may use rituals, spells, or potions to aid their pack.

Silver: A metal that is traditionally harmful or lethal to werewolves. Silver's effects can vary, from causing burns upon touch to being used in weapons designed to injure or kill werewolves.

True Mate: The concept of a predestined, perfect match for a werewolf, often involving a deep, soul-level connection. Finding one's true mate is considered a rare and blessed event, marked by intense emotional and physical bonds.

Ascension: The process by which a werewolf rises in rank within the pack hierarchy, often through challenges, rites of passage, or fulfilling certain conditions set by pack traditions.

Bonding Ceremony: A formal ritual that solidifies the mate bond between werewolves, often involving specific vows, exchanges of gifts, or communal acknowledgment by the pack. It may also involve magical or spiritual elements to strengthen the bond.

Call of the Wild: An instinctual urge that drives werewolves to embrace their wolf nature, often leading them to seek solitude in nature or engage in traditional werewolf behaviors. This call can be powerful during lunar events.

Dominance: A social hierarchy principle within werewolf packs, where individuals assert their power and status over others. Dominance can affect pack dynamics, leadership succession, and mate selection.

Elders: Senior members of a werewolf community who are respected for their wisdom, experience, and often their powerful abilities. Elders may serve as advisors, mediators, or leaders in spiritual or mystical practices.

Full Moon Fever: A colloquial term describing the heightened state of aggression, power, or restlessness that werewolves experience during the full moon. This period can challenge a werewolf's self-control and amplify their instincts.

Heir: A werewolf designated to succeed the current alpha, often their offspring or a chosen successor. The heir is usually groomed for leadership through training, education, and by taking on responsibilities within the pack.

Kinship Bond: A deep, familial bond that connects members of a werewolf pack beyond simple pack dynamics, emphasizing the concept of the pack as a family unit. Kinship bonds enhance loyalty, empathy, and cooperation among pack members.

Lycanthropy: The condition or ability to transform from human to wolf, typically seen as a supernatural trait or curse. Lycanthropy can be hereditary, transmitted through bites, or bestowed through magical means.

Moon Ceremony: A ritual performed by werewolves in honor of the moon, particularly during full moon phases. These ceremonies can involve offerings, prayers, or celebrations of the werewolf's connection to lunar power.

Pack Law: The set of rules and traditions that govern the behavior and organization of a werewolf pack. Pack laws address issues such as leadership, territory, conflicts, and the treatment of outsiders.

Primeval Forest: Mythical or sacred woods that are ancient and untouched by human civilization, often serving as a sanctuary or power source for werewolves and other supernatural beings.

Quarry: In the context of werewolf hunts or challenges, the target or prey a werewolf or pack is pursuing. The quarry can be a creature, a rival werewolf, or an object of significance.

Rune Magic: A form of mystical practice that involves the use of ancient symbols or runes believed to hold magical powers. Werewolves or shamans may use rune magic for protection, healing, or enhancing abilities.

Spirit Walk: A mystical journey or meditation practice that allows a werewolf to connect with their inner spirit, ancestors, or the natural world. Spirit walks can offer guidance, healing, or insight into personal or pack issues.

Totem: A symbolic object, animal, or figure representing a werewolf or pack's spirit, ancestry, or guiding principle. Totems are often revered and can play a role in rituals and ceremonies or as a source of power.

Veil: A symbolic barrier that separates the mundane world from the supernatural or magical realms. The veil can hide werewolves and other beings from human detection or refer to the threshold between life and the afterlife.

Alpha Challenge: A formal contest or duel in which a werewolf challenges the current alpha for leadership of the pack. Depending on pack traditions, this test can be based on physical strength, cunning, or even magical prowess.

Beast Within: The primal, animalistic aspect of a werewolf's nature, often associated with their wolf form. Managing the beast within is a central challenge for many werewolves, balancing their human intellect and emotions with their more instinctual urges.

Crescent Bond: A mystical connection that forms between werewolves who are neither mates nor kin but have forged a bond through shared experiences or battles. This bond is named for the crescent moon, symbolizing growth and potential.

Dire Wolf: A mythical or legendary variant of the werewolf, often depicted as larger and more powerful than standard werewolves. Dire wolves are revered or feared and may have unique abilities or roles within werewolf lore.

Eclipse Ritual: A rare ceremony performed during a lunar or solar eclipse, believed to grant werewolves extraordinary powers or insights. These rituals are often shrouded in secrecy and can have significant consequences.

Fenrir's Kin: A term referencing descendants or followers of Fenrir, the monstrous wolf of Norse mythology. In werewolf stories, Fenrir's kin may possess unique traits or a destined role in werewolf prophecies.

Guardianship Pact: An agreement where a werewolf pledges to protect a human, place, or object, often forming a magical bond that grants the guardian and their charge special protections or abilities.

Harmony Howl: A communal howling session that serves to strengthen pack bonds, communicate over long distances, or celebrate significant events. Harmony howls are deeply spiritual and can have healing properties.

Instinct Awakening: The moment a young or newly turned werewolf first experiences the full force of their werewolf instincts, often during their initial transformation. This awakening is a rite of passage and can be both exhilarating and terrifying.

Lunar Grace: A blessing or state of enhanced agility, beauty, or charisma attributed to the moon's influence on werewolves. Lunar grace can be temporary or permanent, depending on the individual's connection to the moon.

Moon Guardian: A title or role within some werewolf societies overseeing rituals, ceremonies, and the interpretation of lunar omens. Moon guardians are deeply respected and considered vital to the spiritual health of the pack.

Night Veil: An ability or spell that allows werewolves to move unseen or undetected during the night. This ability can be natural, a learned skill, or a gift from the moon or a deity.

Omega Rising: The rare event where an omega werewolf rises to challenge and potentially overthrow an alpha, often seen as a sign of major change or upheaval within the pack.

Pact Mark: A physical or magical mark signifying a werewolf's allegiance to a pact, person, or cause. Pact marks are binding and carry significant weight in werewolf culture.

Quell: A command or ability to suppress or calm the beast within, either within oneself or in others. Quelling is valuable, especially in maintaining secrecy or situations requiring restraint.

Rune Fang: A mythical weapon or tool, often a tooth or claw, inscribed with runes to enhance its power. Rune fangs are rare and highly sought after for their magical properties.

Shadowmeld: An ability allowing a werewolf to blend into shadows or darkness, becoming nearly invisible. Shadowmeld is helpful for stealth, spying, or escaping danger.

Wolf's Bane: A plant or substance known to weaken or repel werewolves. Similar to nightshade or silver, wolf's bane is often used in potions or barriers against werewolves.

www.ingramcontent.com/pod-product-compliance
Lightning Source LLC
Chambersburg PA
CBHW070503170726
48291CB00008B/2638